Giraudoux, Jean, 1882-1944
Lying woman: a novel. Translated from the French by Richard Howard. N.Y., Winter House Ltd. [c1972]

Originally published in French in 1969 under the title: La Menteuse.

I. Title
LW 2/72

78-185598

JG

Translated from the French

by RICHARD HOWARD

Winter House Ltd New York

LYING WOMAN : A NOVEL

BY JEAN GIRAUDOUX

First American Edition
Translation by Richard Howard

Library of Congress
Catalog Card Number 78-185598
ISBN 0-87806-017-0

The Publisher of this edition
wishes to thank Nathan Gross

Manufactured in
The United States of America

1

Reginald avoided women. Not because he disliked them. But he may have been more sensitive than his friends to this fact: at a certain age, a man ceases to be the hunter; he has become the quarry. Once he is over forty, women throng to rescue from death whatever tenderness, wisdom and strength a man still contains. They line up, they pursue him; when they sew him in his shroud, they want to lay out a body exhausted, a soul extinguished *for them.* There were even times when Reginald noticed in himself—did this not justify such pursuit?—a reluctance to stand by and watch while his accumulated stores of justice and intelligence and affection grew old unsuspected, unappreciated. Social quality is greatly heightened by the presence at the dinner table of an archduke incognito, even if mistaken for a banker; and moral quality, by the presence of a soul that claims to be perfunctory and teems with generosity and devotion, even if unemployed.

But women saw no use in Reginald's generosity and devotion serving the world's elevation in general rather than theirs in particular. If the fact that Reginald never closeted himself with a woman conferred upon the universe a special warmth and polish, as his friends claimed, then imagine the polish and warmth conferred upon the woman with whom he might yet closet himself! So they would manage to closet themselves with *him,* setting the kind of trap tigers and elephants fall into, impaled upon a stake—inviting him to meet friends who had not been invited, to visit the studio of a painter who had been asked to stay away for the afternoon, and the stake was planted—even in the studio (the painter, who wanted his work admired, would have been furious!)—by that dim light appropriate for seances but prescribed as well for apparitions of the real. These women did not reckon with Reginald's skill—he never abandoned hope that the missing friends would arrive at any moment, he talked about them, made them the cause of the occasion, made them *present*—nor with his talent for discovering, just inside the studio door (in order to admire the paintings) a light switch. It would really have taken a deep pit in the heart of the jungle, and a cloudy night as well: who knows what else he might have thought of by starlight. Worst of all, he never gave any impression of being sickly—hand-to-hand, for instance, there would have been no hope of defeating him—or of detesting love. It was horrible, that kind of sanctification he cast over you, especially since he seemed anything but invulnerable. In fact he seemed weak, susceptible . . . It was the fault of that armor he was wearing. Invisible armor. For Reginald was everything you could want in a man, not silly, not crude, the ideal man before love, the ideal man afterwards. Why was love missing? There ought to be a law forbidding the few men one thinks of as real men to shirk their duty.

Reginald shirked nothing. Nor was he unaware of his worth as a man. He knew that he carried happiness in his heart, the secret of happiness, and that he could give some woman the advantage of it. All the skirmishes of war, the discords of peace, the triumphs and defeats of commerce, in which he had widely participated, had had at least this result: they had formed a man—perhaps the only one, but still there was one—a man worthy of the name. Because Reginald existed, the earth was a well-populated planet. Aside from two minor imperfections—he cried at the theatre and enjoyed crossword puzzles—he had actually attained a slight yet undeniable resemblance to the Being who is supposed to have created us.

He knew all the comforts and stimulants of this life, and he used them sparingly. Nor did this cut him off from other men. He felt a genuine fraternity with them all, good and bad. He was successful, not proud; brave, not vain. Time and again he had had those adventures which are unique in other lives: he had rescued a drowning child; he had been the first man to enter a conquered city; he had informed a queen that she must abdicate at once; he had announced from a balcony that a nation was free; he had stopped the runaway horse of a boarding-school carriage filled with sixteen-year-old girls; he had been gunned down and left for dead. In his hands, all the life which drips from others like sweat had congealed in episodes. Wherever he went, there was a tendency to take him for a king in exile, for a prime minister in office: he was merely a man in office, being with regard to the gifts of civilization what savages are with regard to nature. Intelligence, feeling, enjoyment were given to him not through surrogates but directly—the way the bread tree, the meat tree, and the wine tree give savages bread, meat, and wine. Fluorescence, iridescence, scintillation—such things he understood to perfection. From the view of a landscape Reginald extracted precisely what was chromatic and picturesque about it; from a storm, precisely what was terrifying, granted that the phenomenon is but a movement of the globe and not a celestial maneuver; from a calm sea, precisely what, by whitecaps, gulls, the smoke of steamships, it offers in the way of grandeur and of peace—but without his relation to such spectacles being in the least denatured or stylized. The same was true of his relations with human beings and with animals. No one ever saw better than Reginald what a horse is, its beauty, its arabesque, and what the union of man and horse might be. Dogs and cats accounted him at first glance an honorary member of the race of dogs or cats. It must also be said that life was easier for him by the fact that he was at its mid-point and beginning the descent.

Sometimes he doubted. Sometimes he thought: "I'm just like all the rest." And he would test this human instrument—himself—at its points of resonance to the world, at the loveliest landscapes; or at its points of maximum resistance or weakness, at Schubert, at Poussin. But in each case he was obliged to admit that between the universe and himself there was the same success as between sound waves and the best radio. In order to find the stations, in order to find those generally unrealizable concurrences between the ocean and innocence, between the chateau of Chambord and generosity, between springtime and justice, Reginald had neither to dispute nor to search, but to appear.

Instead of the usual virginity of a young adult male (which he had, moreover, deliberately preserved), Reginald had the virginity of the superior human being he was—and he did not want to discard it at random.

Friends of both sexes nursed ambitions for him, and all of them belabored the same problem. But they all made the same mistake: they were looking for Reginald's equal, and there was no such thing. They were trying to form that ideal couple which the mere sight of him suggested. Ancient ladies, past mistresses of the art of legitimate or illegitimate coupling, would have found all their mistakes justified had they succeeded on this occasion. Some of them tended toward perfect beauty, others toward moral or spiritual perfection. One had almost managed to convince Reginald; to induce him to *think about* a certain young woman everyone adored, and he had seen her, and he had been charmed, and on the very day he was to speak to her, the ancient lady had learned that the girl was entering a convent the next morning . . . "How well she hid her thoughts!" she had told Reginald, "but if she permits you to say goodbye, it means *you* are the one to take her from the world."

She had permitted him. She had permitted him half an hour. The ancient lady left them together, delighted, assured of Reginald's victory over the Other Suitor; she played a hand of bezique with the girl's aunt, promising God a candle if He lost *His* game. And after half an hour the girl came into the room, radiant, almost on Reginald's arm. And as she left the house, the ancient lady had no further doubts, for she noticed a red mark on Reginald's cheek as he opened the car door for her. Faint, for Chantal used very little rouge, only enough so her parents would not think she was anemic and because Christ likes his virgins healthy. But the healthy virgin had kissed Reginald. Yet, the next morning, Chantal entered the convent. For she had hesitated until that last evening only because she found no charm in the world, because she disdained it a little, because she felt a certain cowardice, a certain selfishness about abandoning what is weak for what is beautiful, what is pathetic for what is perfect. And on the day Reginald arrived, Chantal was about to make her great sacrifice: to remain in the world, to play bridge with arthritics, to play tennis with fools, to make conversation with the dumb and see apparitions with the blind.

But the world's last delegate had shown her, in that last half hour, all its beauty and temptation. He had come in gently, had spoken, had remained for a few moments outside her, outside her heart, and she had understood him and opened that heart, and he had entered it. And thenceforth she had something to sacrifice, to escape: a world where there was Reginald. And what she had offered up to God was no longer an insipid life, but life with Reginald. And the human sacrifice she would make, one to wound her in body and soul alike, was Reginald's child. And the little smear of rouge purloined from God was as nothing compared to the blood that glowed in Chantal's face.

And Reginald, for his part, had thought: "What could I add to such happiness? How much better than I God will play the part, typecast in the role of poor divinized human which makes me so appealing to Chantal . . ." He went to bed, protecting the place where she had kissed him, and did not wash it the next morning. About four that afternoon, at which time Chantal, by the way, was already a cloistered novice, he glanced in the mirror and saw that the mark had disappeared. Since then, a reddish shadow sometimes reappeared on his cheek—fatigue or arthritis—and he called that Chantal's Kiss.

For Reginald was not in the least deterred that his heroines were named Chantal or Edwige or even Maleine, and belonged to important families as well. It was not just because of his distaste for proletarian literature, but because for Reginald what was true in the theatre was true in life: Real human conflict begins only with kings, and the soul really belongs only to those who need not bother with their bodies, who have no bodies. Kings, or children. He remembered with awe the greatest love he had inspired. It was in Portugal, at Alcobaça, where two famous lovers are buried; a comfortable Portuguese couple and their eight-year-old daughter were visiting the place, like himself. There had been some confusion at the door, he had taken the child's hand to keep her from being pressed against a wall by the crowd, and she would not let him go. The visit lasted hours. First came the newer buildings, sunny courtyards, libraries with paintings; in one, a little girl was holding the hand of a great haloed saint. The child had pointed to the halo and also to the chain which linked the little girl's hand to the saint's in the painting. In the refectory, there were not enough glasses to go round, and when the visitors tasted the monastery wine, Reginald and the child drank out of the same glass. Her parents smiled, not suspecting their misfortune. Among these tapestries, these marvelous carved or painted figures, in this abundance and this austerity, they became in their beloved daughter's eyes merely earthly, and remote. Then came the climb up to the terrace, by twin staircases which halved the crowd of tourists.

"Let me take her," Reginald said to the parents.

"Take her," the father said . . .

And she was given. And believed herself given forever. Reginald took her in his arms at the steep places. She kissed him. She could not understand what he was saying, for she did not know French. But for lovers, speech is so futile. And they went on into the cloisters where the dead monks lay, visible under their glass panes. And the parents were on the other side of the cloister. They waved from the other side of death. The child replied—she squeezed Reginald's hand harder with her left hand, and with her timidly liberated right hand she waved at those parents of hers who after all had not been so bad, had been good, while she lived with them. Reginald complimented her on her dress, which was yellow with a red belt; she understood the compliments, even in a foreign language; her one regret was to have left in Livia her red dress with the yellow belt. But why regrets! How lucky she was—she had had to wait only eight years to find happiness. That was unusual, for a girl. In front of the lovers' tomb, she listened to the guide, reserved, almost suspicious. She didn't believe all those stories; love is not so rare as all that. Right there in front of this tomb was a couple much more reliable than the horizontal couple inside. Reginald felt this little soul swelling beside him, and he began to be afraid. He was a little harsh once or twice, deliberately. She trembled, suffered, but was only the gentler for it, and he found himself obliged to caress her hair.

During luncheon, the parents were at the far end of the table, chatting with an infantry colonel from the colonies, and laughing. So much the better, if parents who are losing their daughter can so easily console themselves with infantry colonels from the colonies. And finally the time came to leave Alcobaça, and here the two lives diverged: on the one hand, the splendid car, the handsome chauffeur, and the man to whom she had been given for life and to whom she had given herself several times during the afternoon; and on the other, the bus returning to Livia, to the Livia family, to the Livia street with the pharmacy on the corner. And she knew, when Reginald leaned down to kiss her, that he was forsaking her, and she began to cry. And as a matter of fact he was leading her back to her parents. And she struggled, she screamed at her parents that she hated them, at Reginald that she loved him, and she clung to him. The parents tugged at her feet, at her little legs, naked now right up to her belly.

"She's right," Reginald mused. "She's the one who's right. Absence is the only terrible thing in the world—she doesn't want absence. My head next to hers is a not intervene. Monks were asking the policemen what minimum presence . . ."

Reginald dared not be too brutal about unhooking those tiny hands which were choking him, those bare legs which, liberated by kicking, returned to him, straddled him. A crowd had gathered. The policemen dared was the matter.

"It's the little Bentès girl—she doesn't like Livia any more," the policeman explained.

"But it's a nice town," the monk said. "I know the curé—he's a diviner."

"She wants to go in the limousine . . ."

It was not true. She would have gone to Livia—with Reginald; she would have taken the bus—with Reginald; and Livia would have become the loveliest town in the world, and the bus a winged chariot. The parents tugged at their beloved daughter angrily now, they yanked her away. As Reginald was leaving, monks, guards, visitors gathered around a poor yellow heap rolling in the dust screaming meaningless sounds, for Reginald and she had even forgotten to tell each other their names . . .

Reginald often wondered about that name. More than once he had been tempted to write to Portugal: people in Livia would have remembered the scandal, and there were even times when he reproached himself for not having gone to live there with a little girl eight years old. That would be his sin before the Lord, on Resurrection Day . . . But first of all there was the matter of dying. He could have sent her toys, could have received her portrait—in the red dress . . . But who could have consoled her? She was from that province of Portugal where men duel to the death with staves: who would have dueled to the death for her? With her luck, the man she loved would be killed by the other one, would have his teeth chipped, one eye put out . . . Had she finally accepted the other one?

While Reginald strolled along the terrace at Saint-Germain, thinking about his little Portuguese love, Nelly sat disconsolate at the other end. For just as Nelly was leaving her house to spend the day in the country, her cleaning woman had asked her to take along her eight-year-old daughter: it would be a treat Nelly could scarcely deny the child. But when it is so difficult to find love by yourself, it is no joke to go looking for it in a little girl's company. Also, there was a certain hypocrisy about taking this child, who thought she was going on a safari, to no more than a great windswept terrace which reminded you at every moment how near you were to Paris. Lulu, moreover, had guessed: when half an hour had gone by and Madame had not moved from her bench, participating only vaguely in the leopard hunt taking place in the bushes, Lulu guessed Nelly was waiting for someone and demanded to be taken into her confidence.

Who was coming? . . . A friend . . . Someone Lulu knew? . . . No, Nelly herself didn't know if she would recognize him . . . Why not? Had they arranged to meet by letter? Had they met through the correspondence columns in the newspaper? That was how her mother had married a "gentleman, well-off, kindly, generous, and fond of long evenings at the fireside"; this gentleman was Lulu's father who was penniless, got drunk every night, and beat them both before he left for the bistro . . . No, it was some sort of cousin but Nelly was very fond of him; he had rescued her from drowning when she was a little girl . . . Did he love her? . . . Yes, he had promised to love no one else . . . Then how would they recognize each other—by a flower, by carrying a newspaper in one hand? . . . By nothing, but they would recognize each other . . .

Lulu wasn't so sure . . . She asked questions, and

Nelly was glad to plunge the child into an affair which did not yet exist, to have—through Lulu—a proof that it did.

"Here he comes!" Nelly exclaimed. "He's wearing a pink in his buttonhole . . ."

But it wasn't the one—it was Reserve Commander Loribal, walking his chows. Commander Loribal came to a standstill, moreover, in front of Nelly, blocked her view, wondered if he dared to speak, coughed, walked on.

"Here he comes, he's hurrying!" Nelly exclaimed.

And as a matter of fact, from the other end of the terrace strode a man with huge blue eyes, handsome, wearing a frock coat . . . He wasn't the one . . . But suddenly Lulu saw in Nelly's eyes that the right one was coming.

Lulu was sure he would recognize Madame. He had good eyes, no monocle. It was easy, he must have so many memories. Besides, there was no one on the terrace to recognize except Madame. Even the ones who had never seen her—Commander Loribal and the young archivist with the blue eyes—recognized her.

"Did you have a signal?"

"Yes," Nelly said, "I would whistle the first three notes of ship's leave."

"Whistle them now, and he'll come. There he is, don't move."

And the two of them on their bench, squeezed against each other like children playing hide-and-seek in a closet, Nelly's eyes fixed straight ahead, Lulu's rolling back and forth, already heard the gravel crunching under Reginald's feet.

He did not stop or turn aside.

"Wait!" cried Lulu.

"Be still!" Nelly said.

"He's looking at us, at last he's looking at us."

And as a matter of fact, surprised by Lulu's cry, Reginald was looking at them, seemed to recognize Lulu, smiled at her, and walked on.

"The ingrate!" Lulu said. "Are men all like that?"

"Yes," Nelly said, "all except this one."

The remark was a little surprising, but Lulu understood it. "There are men who never manage to recognize faces. It's especially annoying when they're affectionate. They recognize hats, Maman says. What was yours like, the last time he saw you?"

"A feather toque—I'll give it to you tonight if he recognizes me."

"And what dress were you wearing?"

"Gray wool with a little cape: it was winter. You can have that too, if he recognizes me. But it doesn't seem likely."

"We'll see," Lulu said. "I wish I knew how to whistle. How does your signal go? How do you whistle?" And in an instant, though every butcher boy and milkman in her neighborhood had failed to teach Lulu how to whistle, she managed to produce, somewhere between her teeth and her lips, a shrill sound, though she could not give it the tune of ship's leave.

Reginald was already far away.

"He'll recognize you on the way back . . ."

Perhaps, of course. But now it was a question of discovering whether he would come back or stride into the woods.

"He can't stride into the woods, since he has an appointment," Lulu said.

But Nelly had her doubts and indeed Reginald hesitated, at the edge of the oaks. There was something that drew him on, for he stepped into the glade. He was like one of those film characters who have come out of a book and who return to it, once their roles are finished.

"He thinks you're in the woods," Lulu said.

And she uttered a cry. Not the tune of ship's leave, but a cry—the cry by which Lulu, when she went to the grocer's and there was something to tell the little girls in the neighborhood, alerted the concierge's daughters, the two Papaye girls. But the cry of the Papayes had more effect than the song; Reginald turned around —a shimmer of leaves had drawn him into the woods, a child's cry could certainly draw him back out. Especially since it was no ordinary cry. It was a cry combining the *irinzina* Lulu had learned from the Basque butler upstairs and the yodel the Swiss plasterer had taught her.

Reginald came back, passed by again. The little girl who had cried was silent, he smiled at her and walked on.

"Have you changed so much?" Lulu asked.

"Yes," Nelly answered, "ten years ago my hair was blonde."

"But you had the same black eyes—eyes don't change."

"No," Nelly said, "they were bright blue."

"But your teeth, he could tell them a mile away."

"I didn't have many at fifteen—they came in late."

"We really should have the toque and the cape," Lulu said. But she also decided there was a secret. Something was being kept from her. Perhaps Madame and the stroller had agreed, as a sign of recognition, not to recognize each other. "Are you absolutely sure he's the one? Does he have the same eyes, the same hair?"

"Yes, I must have become someone else. You see, he's far away now. He's leaving."

"He's just made the signal."

"No, he dropped a Metro ticket."

"Doesn't he have a car?"

"Yes, he has cars, chauffeurs, race horses, but today he's entrusted himself to the Inferior Powers of the Earth."

"What are the Inferior Powers of the Earth?"

"The ones that take care of ordinary people."

"The Papaye girls and me?"

"Yes, you wouldn't want special roads in the world when you move around, would you?"

"The Papaye girls have a tandem."

"Tandems and tricycles belong to the Inferior Powers of the Earth. So do things you wouldn't believe, like the elevator that goes to the top of the Eiffel Tower. It's a false Superior Power that makes it work. On the other hand, the elevator in the Hotel Crillon belongs to a real Superior Power."

"Couldn't the Papaye girls or I ever use the instruments of a Superior Power?"

"It's very difficult. Some day I'll try putting you on the back of a racehorse."

"I've already been there. My father took me to the stables at Chantilly, his cousin's a groom there. They put me on a mare named Armide. But they didn't let us out of the stall. So that wasn't a Superior Power?"

"Yes, but one that didn't move. Ordinary people find them sometimes—but then they're motionless. You were a good girl that day, weren't you? And you weren't afraid? That's because you were in the life of the Superior Powers."

"Don't let him go. Look, he's going. Are you supposed to meet again?"

"In ten years, every ten years, until we recognize each other. Let him go."

But Lulu didn't want to let him go. She felt somehow that a man and a woman must not waste a minute when they meet and recognize each other. Ten years of joy, of happiness—that counted, even for a little girl like herself.

"You must follow him! Let's follow him!"

Nelly resisted, but the child had already gone. She could not let the child run all the way to Saint-Germain, or into the woods, where the Inferior Powers lurked, inferior to everything. And Lulu cried out, and Reginald, turning back, saw the child pursuing him, and thought he had lost or forgotten something. He had forgotten Nelly. He had lost Nelly. He walked faster toward her, for Lulu was out of breath from running, but she was too late; already she couldn't take another step, she stumbled. There was only one thing left to do: collapse and call for help. Which is what she did, while Reginald and Nelly arrived from opposite directions, running toward the child lying on the gravel and really crying now.

Reginald looked at the child. She was like the little Portuguese girl, she had caught him and would not let him go again.

"What's the matter?"

"You've got to recognize her!"

"Recognize who?"

"She's changed. She doesn't have her feather toque any more, but she's the one!"

"Which one?"

"The one you're looking for. I've got him, Madame, I've got him!"

The child's prisoner, Reginald looked at the young woman coming toward him. He looked at her like a blind man. He didn't recognize her. And Lulu began sobbing.

"What's the matter with her?"

"She wants you to recognize me," Nelly said. "It's a game the stupid child is playing. I don't know what's come over her."

He smiled. He looked at that charming face. He began playing the game.

"What could I have been thinking of," he said. "Of course it's you."

"Yes, she's the one, she is, she is!" Lulu cried.

"What was the child saying—you haven't changed!"

"Only the eyes," Lulu cried, "and the hair . . ."

"How long has it been since I last saw you?"

"Ten years," Lulu said, "and if it hadn't been for me, you'd have had to wait ten more. I'm terribly thirsty, Madame."

He invited them for tea. Then a magnificent automobile drew up alongside the pavilion and drove them back to Paris. Lulu said nothing. There were flowers in the automobile. Everything was leather, velvet, maple, silver and mirrors. Lulu was very good—good enough to fool the Superior Powers of the Earth.

2

Since the readiness with which a woman gives herself to a man proves either her inexperience or her frivolity, it would be simple gratitude for him to interpret it in the first sense. When Nelly had become Reginald's mistress, she held her breath for a week, waiting for a clue from her new friend. There were two solutions: either Reginald would try to find out who she was, and she would have to take steps; or he would not question her, he would let matters turn out as they might, and that too would have to be prevented. But with that birdlike prescience frivolous women have, Nelly came down on neither side, compromised nothing. She never talked about herself, wore no jewelry which seemed to have a story; she even found hats which despite their red, or their green, seemed anonymous. Each time they met at a restaurant, at a theatre, she arrived with the apprehension she would have to reveal to Reginald a past, adventures, a modest life, an ordinary family: this was what she had done with Gaston, who by the second week was no longer unaware of a single one of Nelly's cousins and Nelly's lovers. But a secret anxiety impelled her to have no family, no country, no habits and no vices. She uttered a city's name only if she had been there quite innocently, she mentioned only dogs she had not known or owned herself, she avoided all mention of concerts or musicians she adored, feeling they would be the first to betray her; she avoided thinking of certain friends as she would have avoided the friends themselves. And the results were favorable. Reginald asked no questions. Reginald obviously desired, however unconsciously, not to add to a series but to have, to himself, a new being.

She redoubled her precautions. No allusion was ever made to her relatives, her trips to the country, her studies. She confined herself to a terrain liberated from her previous life, from her previous habits, from her past excursions, from the pleasures and regrets she had had—a virgin terrain. What is there to say of the virginity she rediscovered in Reginald's arms? She renounced experience, she renounced—almost—memories; sometimes she felt so weak, stripped as she was of her life, her eyes would fill with tears.

She had to say this much for Reginald: he set no traps for her. Was it that he understood all women in general and sought to sanctify them by silence, by ignorance? Or was it that he felt reluctant to spoil this grace of their encounter—that he wanted to respect in her, as she respected in him, a kind of incognito? For she was certainly obliged to respect it in him. Loquacious, jealous, inquisitive, she was obliged, in relation to this man she was beginning to love more than she had ever loved before, to hold her tongue, not to speak, and above all not to speak of other women.

These first silent meetings, when neither Nelly nor Reginald asked questions—except about their health, or their love, their rest or their sleep—took her a long time to get used to. In winter she might not have been able to manage it; but it was summer. A certain languor overcame the most garrulous tongues; the breeze failed to wrest the slightest complaint from the roofs, from the trees. So much was unknown, why not lie down before it all, in silence? Whatever expectorations the tree had received from the balcony, whatever bird-droppings and hair-combings and carpet-beatings, it spoke no more than she. But it would have been interesting to know why Reginald was so good at taking you in his arms, so skillful at lifting you off the ground. He did it as if it had been his profession to pick up from the couch burdens weighing one-hundred ten to one-hundred forty pounds and from five to five-and-a-half feet long and to carry them over to the bed. He never made a mistake. The arm was always in the right place, the hand precise. You couldn't suppose he had spent his life in training with mannequins before he met Nelly. There had been a first mannequin to transport—some infamous person—a second, a third. But none that suddenly turned out to be too heavy, none that struggled, or else how could Reginald's face be so confident?

How could she ever find out the names of so many splendid and perfect persons!

There must be no hesitation: a part of her life had better be concealed from Reginald, and a part had to be admitted in their love. After all, Reginald could hardly imagine she had had neither a childhood nor early joys nor a first passion . . . She anthologized from her life—the life of an appealing and frivolous woman—all that was impregnable; there were certain excursions which could be used unaltered, trips she had taken with harmless people; there were cities that emerged pure and sparkling from her past: Annecy, where she had spent one spring by herself (a whole virgin lake, what luck! the swans, the rowing were saved); Amiens, where she had been to a first communion (a cathedral, too, appeared upon the waters); and everywhere, though she had supposed her past compromised by her relationships, there appeared objects, beings, tastes which were hers alone, which nothing had made suspect. She could offer certain paintings, certain books without those fingerprints a detective looks for—the fingerprints of a man; and there were certain authors she had read without advice, not the best ones, but she loved them all the more for having come to her without intermediaries, and she quoted them to Reginald, who laughed at her tastes. With regard to Lulu too—for Reginald often asked about her—there had to be the same winnowing-out; Lulu had to stop being the daughter of the cleaning woman recommended by Gaston's cleaning woman, herself recommended to Gaston by the cook of a certain Hervé whose relations with Nelly were rather undefined. She would have to take steps. In Paris, when Reginald was out of town, she selected new itineraries; one day she went to Belleville, she talked with people who lived in Belleville, she continued on as far as Le Pré Saint-Gervais. Certainly a little girl's babyhood could be established there, somewhere between the peaceful little town and the hills from which you could see Paris. The very monuments supplied her with the texture of a new life, with great men (Richard Lenoir, Blanqui) and events (the Commune, the burning of the Tuileries) that had been spoiled for her by so many visits *à deux* to the Museum of Decorative Arts.

She was wise to be prepared. One day, Reginald spoke. He did not say what she would have liked to hear: "Before us, there was no one; before us, we didn't exist." He did not make matters easy. One day, sprawled in an armchair beside her, he began—though till now their present, their moment, had been eternity—he began to tell her the story of his life. The room was dark. It all seemed less like a confidence than a confession. It was a confession with the tone, with those smiles and self-deprecations which are not allowed in confessionals. Reginald confessed the city where he was born, he confessed his mother, his sister. Nelly listened, embarrassed, and asked questions about Nevers which she could have answered herself, for she had visited the city once with Gaston. She appreciated this gift Reginald was making of himself now, but she would rather he said nothing; she trembled. She was suddenly panic-stricken, for she realized she was not one of those beings who, taking the hand of their beloved, can recite their life as if it were a song, can pick up the refrain at any point in its course and proceed, without receptions, to magnificent melodies.

That was what Reginald did: he sang. He sang the way the bards or the minnesingers were supposed to sing, without music, but without artifice. It was the Song of Reginald she was hearing now, as she might have heard the Song of Roland: when he left his mother for the war, when he discovered Briand, when he had a dog named Pouce that saved him from drowning. His bayonet might have a name, too. His horse. His orderly. Now he stopped singing, but she felt he might resume with the next verse or the preceding one, with the ballad of his boarding school, with the song of his trip to China, or with the Wilson song—when he had been the only man in Versailles willing to ask the American President if the Senate was behind him.

Was this the goal of life—that it could be told like this, that it could be sung? If it was, how few people could start theirs in such an atmosphere, such a fever of heroism which would determine it forever! It was a recipe the parents of heroes teach their grandchildren, but which Nelly's mother, according to whom a girl's entire education consists of wearing gloves, had certainly neglected. Young heroes can fling themselves gloveless into life . . . She had to admit it: the resonance of heroism, of legend, had not echoed in her life until she found Reginald. She had nothing she could tell Reginald but the hours spent with him: a minor couplet.

Perhaps there was a way. Perhaps she could try to make her life—her life up to the time she had met Reginald—the song she might have sung. Perhaps she could find a single meaning, a single color in an existence so miscellaneous, so motley. What were the ingredients of nobility, of legend in her life? What did her memories afford? Nothing very lofty. Quarrels with brothers who themselves had not turned into heroes but silk merchants. Such brothers would have had to be martyrs and apostles at the very least for the loves and wars of childhood to have some interest. The only poet who had written about Nelly had done so one day when they had had to get up early in the morning to take a trip and she had declared she would sleep for a week:

We must awaken our Sleeping Beauty.
Up, men, up, and do your duty.

She was inclined neither to sanctify nor to sin. It was not among women who have statues carved of them, or who are immortalized in novels, that she had to search. She leafed through her photograph album. All the snapshots were there, right from her birth, including the one of the masquerade to which she had come as one of Goya's bulls, and the one of the fake wedding she had attended as the bride—a surprise party for the Speaker of the Chamber of Deputies. She looked at them all, from the naked little girl who innocently exposed her thighs to the young woman who perfidiously concealed them. No, she could not make out the epic of which these photographs were the illustrations. For one thing, she realized that most of them were false: she was on a yacht, or a horse, or a mountain, but she was no more a sailor, a cowgirl, an Alpinist than she was a bull or a bride. They were all masquerades of one kind or another. Photographed in front of Bourges Cathedral, on the site of Joan of Arc's stake, or in front of the world's largest dam, she seemed to be there only to prove that there were beings who have nothing to do with beauty, sanctity, electricity. What a marvelous poet it would have taken to discover a meaning in these images; and worst of all, it was perfectly obvious this was not just a preface, a prologue, but that already Nelly was making her way through life, through a life without songs . . . And that was simply impossible.

One day it occurred to Nelly that if Reginald loved her, he must have heard it—heard her song when she was near him. For now she understood: in all the world, there were only two kinds of beings, those who sang themselves and those who did not. She realized it in her most mediocre friends as well as in the most gifted or the happiest—there were the ones who were their own song, and in whom everything was true, strong, sensitive; and then there were those who copied the songs of the others, poor souls whose youth, whose adventures, whose travels, even whose children were verses detached from other songs and braided into a clumsy garland. The proofs were more numerous than she would have supposed. Lulu had her song which became clearer when, in her shrill voice, she began to sing her life—when her mother tried to make up with her after having spanked her with a slipper:

My mother gave me twenty francs.
I threw it back at her. No thanks.

Among the Italian workmen who came to paint the apartment, one had his song. To match a color, he had painted about twenty samples around a door, and every day he came to paint another. Sometimes he was a little drunk and claimed that the sparrows talked to him on the way . . . "Cheating on you, she's cheating on you," is what the sparrows told him. If the sparrows bothered with that, it must have been because they didn't have much to do. He made them repeat it . . . "Cheating on you," they repeated. No matter how hard he tried to find out what it was that interested the sparrows in this affair, he had no luck. If men are cuckolds, what does that have to do with birds, ostriches or sparrows? . . . "Cheating," they repeated, accompanying him down the Rue Monsieur-le-Prince where he bought his paints. "When I was a boy the sparrows never interfered in such matters . . . doesn't anyone ever cheat on them? Just tell me, is the cuckoo a bird or a horse?" Besides, Eusebia wasn't cheating on him. One day he had found her locked in with the butcher boy. He told her what the sparrows were saying. "Silly," she had said. "Look how nice the butcher boy was with you. If you had caught him up to something—you know how strong and mean butchers are—he would have given you a bloody nose." Whereas, quite the contrary, the butcher boy had shaken his hand after putting back on the apron he had removed because of the heat. You wouldn't believe how heavy a canvas apron can be . . . "Besides, if I was a sparrow, I wouldn't go perching on windowsills to watch what happens in people's houses. Nothing worth watching happens. People wash. People pick their teeth. If I was a sparrow, at least I'd go watch how the rich cheat on each other . . . "Maybe she's not cheating," the sparrows said then, "but you're dumb as they come . . ." So then he had thrown stones at them, and they had flown away. Dumb as he was, he had still found a way of getting rid of the sparrows.

Nelly listened, delighted and saddened. Everything this simple fellow did was imbued with truth, with style —just as much as Reginald's heroic deeds. Neither profundity of mind nor diversity of adventure counted for anything in this partitioning of humanity which seemed to exclude her from the elect. Perhaps even the handsome butcher boy had his song, removing his bloodstained apron to keep it from getting wrinkled and spreading it out on the armchair facing the bed.

And even the beings that did not speak, the trees, the animals, had their song. Her cat, without mewing, by its gestures, its poses, was its own song. And the cedar in the Jardin des Plantes where she had taken Lulu in hopes of running into Eusebia. She found out later that Eusebia went only to places that could be locked, for she was timid. And in the zoo, tigers, lions, even condors were their own song. The hyena was a hideous song. And in all these animals, striped or plain, shaggy or sleek, Nelly tried to discover how it was that Reginald resembled them and she did not. How was it that she didn't resemble the tigress? It wasn't because the tigress had hair all over her body and Nelly had stripes only above her eyes—it was because Nelly labeled her letters and, despite Gaston, would not destroy any of the five or six bundles, the Jerome bundle under the pajamas, the Charlie bundle in the nightgowns, the little Reginald bundle in the handkerchief drawer. How was it that she didn't resemble the tapir? It wasn't because of the creature's sloping forehead and Nelly's incapacity to pick up ants with her nose—it was because of her carefully balanced accounts and her monthly visits to the bank.

There were also sparrows in the Jardin des Plantes, sparrows that followed her but did not speak, but Nelly felt that this was because of her insistence on taking baths. They spoke to Lulu, who was as dirty as an old comb and whom Nelly had to throw into the tub with all her clothes on—otherwise she suspected something and vanished into the coal cellar.

*

*   *

The day came at last when Reginald began to talk about her, and Nelly realized that everything would be ruined.

"Afterwards, I won't say that you're *the* truth, but you are a truth. I know nothing about you. I've asked you nothing because I have the feeling I know it already."

What did he know already—who knew the most secret plots of Venizelos and the undivulged future of nations?

"Suppose I start with some intimate event of your life . . . Suppose I start with your engagement."

Her engagement! She had never thought about her engagement.

"You'd think it would torture me to think about your engagement, about that gift of yourself that you made when you were so young. But after all, it was a long time ago, wasn't it?"

"Oh, yes! I was sixteen. So it was eight years ago."

What was the matter with her, falling into his trap this way? Why did she suddenly let the real Nelly and the false Nelly divide themselves up into two dissimilar people? Reginald was grown-up enough to create his own Nelly by himself.

"Besides—I don't know why—I have the feeling that you didn't love him, that even then you realized you didn't love him."

"Oh, no! I didn't love him!"

That was true. He hadn't existed. But she didn't love him. She was even more certain of the fact that she didn't love him than of the fact that he didn't exist.

"I have the feeling you weren't happy when he took you in his arms."

"Oh, no! I wasn't happy."

Why was she answering questions that weren't being asked? Why was she answering even by a saddened, worried face? Because, actually, there was a first truth, a truth hard to admit, which was that he didn't exist. But once this truth was admitted, all the rest was absolutely true. This fiancé who hadn't existed—she couldn't bear him, she couldn't bear the touch of his hands, she loathed his taste in neckties; and her wedding day, the day of a wedding that hadn't happened, when this idiot who hadn't existed stood beside her—it was all true when she thought of Reginald; she had repulsed him, then she had insulted him, then she had spit in his face, then he had resorted to cunning, it had taken two weeks, Reginald. O Reginald, do you know what it means to resist a husband in the same house for two weeks? . . . Then, one night, oh, it was awful!

"Oh, it was awful!" she heard herself saying aloud. "Just awful!"

"You're thinking about your marriage! My darling, my love! If it hadn't been that beast, it might have been a husband you would have loved, and then you wouldn't be here. Was he much older than you?"

If Reginald didn't know everything already about the real Nelly, how well he knew about the false one, about the one who was in his arms, about the real one after all.

"Much older."

"Your parents wanted you to marry him."

Of course her mother had wanted her to marry him.

"He had a name, didn't he—I mean, a famous name?"

"It matters so little to me."

"A house, even a chateau?"

"Yes, but it mattered so little."

"In Venice? In Trieste?"

Why these references to Italy?

"Around there."

"Is he still there?"

"We never write each other."

And that was how Nelly's song began. It was false. But it was a song all the same. Reginald's sketch of her disturbed her a little, but it really simplified her life and her love. She no longer had to act out for him the role of all women at once, innocent and perverse, bride and divorcée, of those women whose every possibility and every virtue she was obliged to assume in order to please this Reginald who persisted in not asking her specific questions. That broken marriage, that pathetic engagement, that palazzo somewhere between Venice and Trieste (she had an Italian friend, an old Prince Borghese, she would ask him for names and descriptions)—all that set a limit to her task without her having to invent a thing, her task as a woman in love who wants to satisfy the man she loves. This unbearable silence of Reginald's about her previous corporeal experiences, a silence which tormented her, condemned her to a kind of criminality each time they slept together, at least this silence no longer existed. At least he admitted—as he had never seemed to admit, as he had always seemed to want to ignore—that there had been one before him . . . Five or six, the real Nelly said, all appealing, all kind and generous. Only one, the false Nelly said, a beast, a brute.

Finally it all came down to the same thing anyway.

The misfortune was that at night, when she was alone in bed and would try to hear her song, she felt more silent than ever. Nothing in her spoke. Her whole body, her whole soul seemed to be mute.

Nothing spoke but what speaks for itself. Her voice. And all it could utter was one great moan.

3

When she awakened the next day, it was not a moan of this kind which welcomed Nelly into a world already occupied and active. It was a voice which said to her: "Not all your feeling for Reginald is what you call natural affection—you know how much of it is the result of your mother's ultimatum . . ."

There may seem to be a good many voices in this narrative. But the truth is, each of us has several voices. To read novels or tragedies is to hear just one voice of characters who would be comprehensible only if all their voices were heard. There is a second part to the role of Phèdre, a second part to Cleopatra, perhaps a third as well. Because these parts are missing, the roles are literature, not humanity . . . Nelly herself had not only those two voices already familiar to us, the voice of imagination and the voice of her lie. She also had a voice which rarely spoke but never failed to intervene, peevish and abrupt, when she was about to deceive herself—a voice which spoke to reinstate the truth. It was hard to tell if the voice spoke for Nelly's own good or to satisfy some thirst for revenge; in any case it had the audacity to speak aloud, not to be just an interior apostrophe. It was this voice which made Nelly say, quite clearly, when she came home from a day with Reginald, happy, proud of him and proud of this love, "and don't forget the jewels he gave you today—they're enormous." The voice even ventured to speak of a particular jewel it called the square diamond. "What about the square diamond—did you get it?" Nelly heard herself ask this dreadful question aloud on the street, and blushed. Or when she took her docile part in a wedding or a funeral, for Nelly was very much a formalist, and when she tried to feel sympathy or joy for the fate of those concerned, an usher could have heard her say about the late lamented: "Will he be as nasty dead as he was alive?", or about the bride: "It's always the dumb ones who get the square diamonds." That was the voice which told her this morning that her feelings for Reginald were the result of her mother's ultimatum.

Moreover it was true. The document she and her brothers called their mother's ultimatum had been found in their father's safe when they opened it after his death. It was a terrifying document which her brothers had ridiculed but which had in fact made Nelly into a person scrupulous toward all humanity, rich and poor alike. After a separation which her father could not endure, for he loved his wife, and which he did not understand, for he had done nothing wrong and she herself had not left him for another man, he had finally obtained an ultimatum: his wife consented to return to his house, but on thirty-one conditions, each of which constituted the subject of a paragraph.

These were the dreadful thirty-one commandments of married life. —*When you tie your necktie in front of my mirror, you will not wiggle your Adam's apple and make little grunting noises.* —*When we sit down at table, you will not stick your hand into your pants pocket and pull out old toothpicks and breadcrumbs.* —*When we walk past the Trocadero, you will never again say: "It's beginning to have a style of its own."* —*You will keep your middle fingernail, the one that has grooves in it, out of my sight.* —*You will not wear resoled shoes, they always squeak on the vestibule tiles.* —*You will never repeat in my presence that story about the man with a sore throat who goes to the doctor and the doctor's wife answers the door.* —*When you take your bath, you will not sing under any circumstances whatever.* —*When you have decided to spend the night in my room, you will never ask: "Would you like me to sleep with you, darling?" You know I wouldn't and that I do so by obligation and on account of the Sacrament. So shut up about it.* —*And on those occasions, you will never have a matching handkerchief in your pajama-top pocket.* —*You will remove from your signature that ridiculous paraph you always add underneath.* —*You will on no account make me admire your dog, and you will on no account tell the dog to admire me.* —*You will take half as long as you do now to brush your teeth, and you will get rid of that effervescent toothpaste. The thought that you are in this very house with a mouth full of foam is absolutely intolerable. —You will quote no Latin phrases or proverbs. You will never again say:* "Chi lo sà," *the only Italian words you know, moreover. —You will never again use the word cubic instead of the word cubist . . . Moreover, once and for all, you will never again discuss painting* . . . And it went on. And there were only thirty-one commandments because, by her antipathies, her inattentions, she had limited her spiritual and visual contacts with her husband to thirty-one.

Moreover her father had agreed to it. Nelly remembered that return, and how empty he had seemed to her; which is to say that he was emptied of thirty-one eccentricities. And indeed he no longer told the story about the man with a sore throat. Nelly had heard someone ask for it at the dinner table one day, and her father had turned beet red. He brushed his teeth in secret, after her mother had gone out. Nelly remembered how he had taken her to the aquarium in the Trocadero one day, and had told her, standing across the street from the building, "Look, Nelly, it used to be ugly, but now it's beginning to have a style of its own . . ." What a style he was beginning to have, that poor father of hers, according to this document! She still had the sky blue handkerchief he had given her once when he came to kiss her good night, and which she had long refused, for her father was wearing sky blue pajamas. He had slid it under her pillow without a word; she had kissed him good night, and he had tiptoed toward her mother's room, palpitating, but mute . . .

"And those are the ones who give girls square diamonds," the voice concluded. He had in fact given a square diamond. On his wife's birthday, she had found the case, had picked it up and asked what it was, and he had swallowed a *Chi lo sà* which gave him a coughing fit and worked havoc with his Adam's apple . . . And this was the woman, too, who had subsequently married a bearded little Deputy with dirty fingernails, a peculiar smell, colored trousers and black jackets, whom she adored and who never stopped telling the story about a chastity medal, compared to which the one about the man with a sore throat was a Viking saga.

Nelly was seventeen when the safe had been opened in order to learn her father's wishes for his funeral, and it was she who had read the ultimatum first. Certain commandments were underlined in red, with a question mark—the ones which he had not understood or which were too unfair, the one about the grooved fingernail, the one about the hair in his ears, the one about the dog, the one prohibiting Russian cologne (she would have preferred iodoform) . . . Through the study door, Nelly saw her father laid out on his bed, his hands folded on his chest, the grooved fingernail terribly noticeable, it was true, for the candlelight glittered on it. At last he was in a state that could please her mother.

The Adam's apple was motionless. No toothpick to fear. A whiff of phenol. So tightly clamped were those jaws that it was quite impossible for certain words to escape from them, words like "Would you like me to sleep with you, darling . . ." A suit without a pocket handkerchief. So his wife had kissed him. She had carried magnanimity to the point of not getting rid of the dog that whined in the next room, the dog that loved all those forbidden gestures. And it was from that day, perhaps, that Nelly had begun to be a conscious human being.

This consciousness impelled her, moreover, to a single duty: not to be importunate to humanity. At first, to avenge her father, she had observed her mother. Nelly had a critical eye—she had inherited it from her mother herself. And for two weeks she had noted all her mother's foibles, had elaborated a new list of commandments which she planned to type up and enclose in an anonymous letter. She did not persevere in this resolve. Her mother's imperfections soon came to seem, on the contrary, the only reasons Nelly would ever have to love the woman. Her phobia about lace—no more lace pillowslips; her nausea about brushing her teeth in Lavoris—no more Lavoris in the house; her mania about using collyrium by the bottle (my eyes smart, my pupils are too big); all these constituted precisely the memories which would touch Nelly most, once her mother was dead.

She had torn up her document . . . But she had decided, for her own part, to offer no further accommodations to either the aversions or the sympathies of humanity. In everything which concerned her own appearance, there would be nothing which could allow another human being to hate or love her too closely. She used lipstick, blew her nose, sneezed, she had ways of wearing stockings, of talking, of writing: in short, an envelope which could neither surprise nor offend. She modified her handwriting—too spidery—to spare some reader or some postman his condescension. And the same was true of all the "outsides" of this envelope . . . Lipstick removed, and in stockings and in garters . . . Even stark naked. Her nails, her hair, had something perfect about them which declined interest or affection. And gradually, in all her gestures, all her actions, Nelly had become more distinct, purer. That charming poet who tried so hard to make friends with her, Francois Grenadin, had told her she was classical. And he was right. She had become, in the way she washed her hands, or her body, or brushed her teeth—above all in the way she brushed her teeth—in the way she ate, or peeled an orange, or dissimulated her perspiration, her fatigue, her saliva, in her way of not wrinkling her dresses, not snagging her stockings—eminently classical. And she had even resumed the habit imposed by her mother of always wearing gloves, for she had finally understood the significance of that commandment: gloves spared her mother the necessity of touching her father. They spared Nelly the necessity of touching humanity. "When you go out with bare hands, it means they have some work to do," the voice said aloud, through Nelly's mouth. And it added: "You'll see, you'll take your glove off soon enough, once the square diamond comes."

This was not quite accurate. The truth is that Nelly was approaching that moment which comes, one day or another, in the life of every man and every woman, the moment which makes that life either justified or *manquée*. It is a moment which can come in extreme youth or in extreme age; it is a kind of grace, which is not the grace for the life to come, but for life in this world. Children of six have received it, one day out walking, closing their eyes under a kiss, getting up on a donkey or walking into a palace. Till now, it had not come to Nelly. No pressure from the outer world, no reading, no music had ever given her that rape, the only true loss of virginity in this world by which every human being is ravished from a virgin humanity and made to stand in line after Mozart, Manon Lescaut, Nero or Colette's first husband. Nelly felt this, dimly. She felt that there was something to do or to suffer in this moment. She suspected it would come just where it most often does, from her lover's face, from a starry sky, from terraces, but, selfish as she was, not knowing if she would encounter joy or disaster in it, she only ventured into such places when Reginald could accompany her. No more music without him, no more boat rides by moonlight, no more organ recitals in cathedrals without Reginald. He was the only one who could protect Nelly against herself. She looked at him face to face, and that face—so dangerous when it was far away—became harmless. Yes, there was one means of never being approached by Reginald—it was to have him, always, there.

*

* *

Nelly felt, then, that she was approaching a maturity, a completeness which affected not only her clothes, or those ornaments of detail which were her eyes or her feet. She was merely, now, as the couturiers say, an *ensemble*. It was easy enough to see, moreover; her friends were amazed, not at failing to recognize her but on the contrary at recognizing her too much, at finding suddenly raised to a higher power in Nelly that rather insipid Nelly they had always seen, always known. "What's come over you?" her mother would ask. "You're just right!" And Nelly suddenly saw in her mother's eyes that hard stare which had instigated the thirty-one commandments, but which found nothing in Nelly. And whereas Nelly had always enjoyed herself more with men who appreciated her specialties—her eyes, precisely, or her fingers, or her teeth—now she preferred men who appreciated her in her entirety, and she gradually changed her admirers, avoiding gigolos in order to make closer contact with men susceptible to beauty in general—*i.e.,* cavalry generals, professors at the Faculty of Medicine, and also children.

"What perfect bearing!" said the cavalry generals.

"A charming person," said Professor Gonzelve.

"How beautiful you are, Madame," said Lulu.

Her entire appearance was ruled now by the desire which Nelly thought was the desire to be admired, but which was in fact the desire to be approved. She took fewer taxis now. This was because she needed to be approved by people walking, by waiters on café terraces, by workmen. Many approved. "A pretty girl," they said. "I'd like a sister like that," said the man who came to read the gas meter to Lulu's mother. Nelly cheated a little—she arrived with a bunch of violets which she told Reginald a young man had just bought at a flower stall and had thrown into her taxi when it stopped for a light. This was not true, it was simply a lie meant to start the siphon between that general approbation she desired and herself. She told Reginald that on her last trip to Spain she had come out of a church and a child had shouted, "Call the curé, the Virgin's clearing out." In short, Nelly tried to obtain from everyone what it had never before occurred to her to ask of anyone, an agreement which was becoming indispensable to her, an acquiescence in her life.

*

*   *

Once, Grenadin had telephoned: the happiest day of his life, he said, would be the day Nelly and Helene Guise came to see him. He had happened to catch sight of them walking together in the street, and as a matter of fact, on that day Helene Guise and Nelly had really looked like two goddesses. They would find him at the Ministry of Labor, where he was an under-secretary of the cabinet. He had just sent his latest book to both women; it was not about a woman, but about a sea lion. Nelly preferred that. Moreover, when a poet can speak in such a way about a sea lion, can make it into such a cunning and impassioned creature, can lodge so much tenderness in flippers, in a fish tail, what might he not do with Nelly, with those false flippers of Nelly's called hands, with that false tail of Nelly's called legs, with those ears of Nelly's which perfectly recalled the sea by their conchlike perfection? And so, with Helene Guise who looked more like a sea horse, Nelly set off for Grenadin as though for an ideal photographer.

It was a beautiful June afternoon. The day's radiance penetrated even the Ministry's long corridors. It was a pair of goddesses who strode down the Avignon carpeting. They climbed the monumental staircase like vacationing caryatids under the admiring gaze of attachés. From the official building there rose, already, an official acquiescence in so much youth and beauty. The ushers' uniforms, the discreet and inquisitive glances of typists, the helmet of a municipal guard, were almost, in this sunlight, the true poetic preparations. They reached the Minister's floor and, turning down the corridor, unaware that the little Louis XVI door under two interlaced naiads was the door to the washroom, continued walking toward it, when suddenly it opened. They had time to hear a toilet flushing, to glimpse

François Grenadin, still slightly unbuttoned, open the door wide, then slam it shut, remaining still inside. Then, giggling, they managed to discover his office where they waited for him. Monsieur Grenadin was busy with the Minister, his assistant said. He would inform Monsieur Grenadin they had arrived.

The assistant returned. "Grenadin isn't here," he said. "He won't be here all afternoon."

They laughed and said where they had seen him.

"He won't come back," the assistant said. "You took him by surprise, and he's embarrassed."

"Please ask him to come back. Tell him we're waiting for him."

The assistant went out again, and they followed him—at a distance.

"Are you in there, François?"

"Where do you think I am? Where else do I deserve to be?"

"Those ladies are waiting for you."

"Tell them I'll never leave this place again. I spend a year daydreaming about them, and this is where they find me."

"You're perfectly entitled to spend a minute in there."

"A minute. Fifteen minutes. I'm a wretch, a miserable wretch. Tell them I'll never see them again."

The assistant returned. "I'll send the usher," he said, "I'll tell him to say the Minister wants him."

The usher came. A good man who was glad to

undertake the mission, but who was incapable of lying. "The Minister wants you, Monsieur Grenadin."

"Tell him where I am."

"It's urgent, Monsieur Grenadin."

"Tell the Minister how lucky he is, Houlier my friend, to have something urgent to do. I'm always idle and useless."

"You're joking, Monsieur Grenadin."

"Houlier my friend, I know the Minister doesn't want me. You're trying to get me out of my refuge. I'm fine in here. And I can see down into the garage through the dormer. Fascinating."

"Monsieur Grenadin, what should I tell those ladies?"

"Houlier, if two ladies you had been dreaming about for over a year suddenly surprised you as you came through this door, in the uproar of a waterfall, would you speak to them calmly?"

"I would be obliged to do my duty, Monsieur François."

"You called me François—that's very decent of you, calling me by my first name in such circumstances. Your name is Ernest, isn't it?"

"My name is Ernest."

"All right, Ernest my friend, no use going on with it. Tell those ladies I'm with the Minister."

"They won't believe it, Monsieur François."

"Ernest—it makes me feel better, calling you Ernest—it doesn't surprise me that they won't believe it. They understand everything. My foolishness, my clumsiness, my destiny to fail—they understand it all, in this one moment. They're lovely, aren't they?"

Ernest glanced at the assistant, who nodded. "I'm not much of an expert in these matters, Monsieur François, but they do seem to be very lovely."

A long silence. Ernest returned, apologized, Helene Guise and Nelly were already at the door. They knocked.

"Now what, Ernest?"

"It's not Ernest," Nelly said, "it's Nelly. Come on out. Come see us."

"You! Never. Leave!"

"But it's so childish of you. I have a brother who goes where you are now every ten minutes."

"So do I. I have a sister who reads the newspaper in here. So what? You don't read anything in here, you —you don't appear in this setting at all."

"It's true that we're lovely," Helene said.

"Take advantage of it, it doesn't happen to us every day."

"I don't care, I'll never see you again."

Nelly grew angry. "Now listen to us! We need you —Helene and I need you. Open that door right now and come to dinner with us. We'll take you wherever you like. And any day this week you choose, we'll be at your disposal."

"I'm no longer good for anything. I'm staying here forever. I'm going to write graffiti on the walls. It's the fate I deserve. I was wondering why my name was

Grenadin. Why I had that stupid name. Now I know."

"You're ridiculous. I'm going to lock you in and take away the key."

So Helene and Nelly were obliged to do without a poet that day. Grenadin did not suspect he had just denied them the world's acquiescence in their life. They supposed he came out, eventually—they never saw him again.

It was after this incident that there appeared in Nelly a kind of complicity with ordinary people, the ones her mother called "the scum." No longer seeking compliments from her peers or from men she had no desire to interest, Nelly reserved all her airs and graces for a subaltern world. She approached laborers half-buried in ditches, she listened to compliments rising from sewer grilles. She went out of her way to appear at political rallies, demolition sites, places where road work was being done. Among taxi drivers, she recognized at a glance the one who would tell her, as she got out of the car, that he had just driven his loveliest customer of the day. Errands to the grocery, the dry goods store, which Lulu was quite qualified to run, gave Nelly the opportunity to prove to those modest women their sorority with this charming, elegant, but modest woman. Bicyclists in red-and-green-striped jerseys brushed against her as they passed, sometimes with their hands. This was not quite what she would have chosen, of course. Sometimes, on her way to Reginald, although she had harvested the sympathy of the "scum" all afternoon, as well as of second fitters and assistant manicurists and Metro ticket punchers, Nelly did not feel at all clear, at all pure, she felt around her both that silence of her own—no song—and the silence of a great voice.

She was like everyone, except for a few. She needed some great praise.

Occasionally Nelly tried to supply it herself. Since Reginald was not a poet—women who have poets for friends have no idea how lucky they are—she tried to see herself as he might have seen her . . . Once or twice in her life she had spoken to herself that way, in the evening, when the lights were dim, while she caressed herself and complimented herself . . . She tried to do it again now, before falling asleep. She began with all the virtues. "O you're so lovely, so kind, so generous, O you always return good for evil . . ."

But not all of it was true. This was the first time Nelly realized that there were even lies in it.

Yet that was the whole problem: to find some great praise for this little person who was, after all, rather mediocre.

4

Gaston's reappearance did not simplify matters.

Not because it was impossible to divide her normal life between him and Reginald. The care she had taken to conceal her new lover surprised Nelly herself. Reginald was the kind of man women boast about, she was keeping a square diamond in the dark. To make a secret—an aberration or a sin—out of what might have been, openly, the most charming and flattering friendship, to make him secret, and herself too—Nelly had sometimes wondered why. Now that Gaston was here, in front of her, jubilant because the International Rice and Cereal Conference of which he was vice-president had spared him two months of America, Nelly wondered which man she wanted to keep from the other, which one made her adopt this double life: in short, which one she loved. She loved someone, she could tell by a certain impatience, a certain uneasiness. A betrayal was involved.

But she wondered who was—who would be—betrayed. Gaston did not suspect that on the pretext of the headache she had invented Nelly was studying him, trying to see whether he was the victor or the victim in the case. It was not even that simple. If she loved Gaston a lot and Reginald a little. Or Gaston a little and Reginald a little less. Even now she realized she did not love Gaston a lot, but that failed to settle the question. Despite all her efforts, there was a kind of equivalence between her non-love for Gaston and her affection for Reginald. Or rather that wasn't where the conflict was; she had never had two lovers at the same time, but like all women her morality was based on a commitment to love, an implicit conviction that even the most modest love takes precedence over everything else, deserves every sacrifice. The conflict was between one man who had several names linked together by hyphens, who could talk about their friends—friends with names—who touched each bibelot, greeted each painting, and another man who shared her life without a human name or a familiar object ever distracting them.

Nelly could answer for her soul. She knew she could endure Gaston's return without the misgivings she might have suffered in the past. So much for the soul. That was all well and good . . . For the body, for the body, that was obviously going to be more painful to discover.

"I know you've been faithful to me," Gaston said, affecting gaiety but visibly moved. "Thank you."

"You've . . . asked people?"

"Oh no. People wrote . . . And I can see."

He saw clearly. Nelly had absolutely no impression of having deceived Gaston. You could deceive Gaston only by loving Gastons, that race of men like Gaston and not like Reginald, a race which includes, in short, all men except one. Between that anonymous, almost unknown body she confided to Reginald for embraces without detail and that inventoried body Gaston knew so well, there was the same difference as between the two souls. But there must have been something more serious, for her sincere and nasty voice began speaking: "Go on. The amnesia trick will do it."

Gaston walked up and down, told about the elevator strike in New York, mixed cocktails, stopped to come over to Nelly and kiss her.

"What's wrong with me!" Nelly was thinking. "Gaston's return isn't going at all the way I thought it would. I'm not sorry to see him—he's even improved. I listen to him, and he's more amusing and more intelligent than I thought he was. His is by far the best version I've heard of the elevator strike in New York. And he seems more sensitive—he didn't even go to his mother's before coming to see me. And he's more serious. And more energetic than I thought he was. Still, all this progress, all this elevation to a higher rank of humanity makes him less precious to me, less agreeable than the Gaston I expected—that frivolous, pot-bellied mama's boy. And he only takes one cocktail now. So why am I upset, when I should be so pleased?"

She was upset, she discovered, because this transfigured Gaston did not make her task an easy one. Women can compromise only with mediocrity. And doubtless if Gaston had returned the same man he was when he left—casual, frivolous, selfish—Nelly would have had little choice. She would have accepted her habitual life with him all over again. But by improving, Gaston emerged from the conditions and from the existence in which compromise and mediocrity are natural.

"How strange!" Nelly mused. "If Gaston were crude, obese, greedy, we would have spent the night together . . . Now I hesitate. The poor boy has no notion what's in store for him, with his loving eyes, his livelier talk, his loyal face!"

Nelly's past had made her a kind of pledge that she would remain ordinary, obtuse, banal—banal. The pledge had been remarkably well kept by her other friends, of both sexes. It was an absolutely indispensable condition, if her life with Reginald was to remain what it was, lofty, silent, at an altitude where Nelly sometimes found herself short of breath. Reginald, of course, could stay what he was wherever he happened to be—he was used to it. But as she was now, Nelly could not. For a few hours a day she could manage that strange, pure reality whose texture she did not yet apprehend, and which was nothing less than generosity, nobility, and love—yes, she could manage. She was natural, happy. But—was it because she decided her other life would be spoiled by this one?—she let none of it spill over into the other hours of the day. Once, when she was getting ready to meet Reginald, it occurred to Nelly that she was dressing like those women who meet their lovers in a hotel, in a *maison de rendezvous.* The same neutral clothes, the same mask of idleness, the same effort to be neither hurried nor deliberate. But Nelly's rendezvous was with a series of habits and ideas which were also alien to her existence, and which were devotion, composure, fidelity. She did not yet feel strong enough to admit these strangers into her house, into her family.

She needed to feel isolated, impervious in her bed, at night, to read the book or listen to the record Reginald recommended, to admit even an echo of life with Reginald. We protect ourselves as best we can. Nelly, until that happy day, protected herself against nobility by a selfish and querulous mother, by small-minded and garrulous friends, by assiduous evenings in Montmartre and a serious attendance at the races. She even followed the trotting races at Vincennes in order to perfect her contact with the "scum." Sometimes a vague melancholy overtook her when she left Reginald —she could not erase the smile of farewell from her lips. This was rare. No Ondine recovering from her marine metamorphosis, no middle-class woman returning from her *maison de rendezvous* ever managed so well to shed the last scales from her legs, to conceal the broken garter in her bag. No sooner was Nelly in the taxi than she took out her perfume and effaced that lack of scent, chatted with the driver to dissipate that silence, and no sooner was she back in her apartment than she began telephoning, trying on dresses, performing life's real occupations, so that nothing should subsist of that other life which she did not know whether to call truth or falsehood.

Yet Gaston, all of a sudden, no longer seemed to abide by this pledge to banality, facility, and mediocrity, which all the others so tenaciously kept. He no longer poked her shoulder a little coarsely, he glanced at her almost timidly, there was something abashed, something considerate about him, like a man who has betrayed. He had betrayed vulgarity, childishness, superficiality. He was not proud of himself. Nelly, enduring her fake headache, watched him and felt thwarted, though uncertain if she was thwarted in a secret or in a privilege. There was worse to come. Gaston treated her exactly as if he had known that she too, during his absence, had become remarkable, perfect, splendid. No longer that fraternal way of nudging her, of addressing her familiarly; it was as if he had seen through some keyhole the arrivals and the farewells in Reginald's apartment; it was as if he knew that two people can look at one another a long time, tenderly, that they can hold one another's hands and say nothing, sit down at a window, one head resting on a neighboring shoulder, that you can rest your lips on other lips without its being a kiss, that you can turn around in the car to gesture to someone watching you leave, a simple gesture—a gesture of the eyelids which makes the universe blink . . . Gaston knowing all this—it was unendurable!

This was not precisely what Gaston knew. But Gaston knew what men like himself, men immersed in business, who have accustomed their friends to seeing them as brutal and immediate creatures with whom a minimum of human relations suffices, did not really have to know. Far away in that exotic country where he had gone to monopolize his bananas and pineapples, he had suddenly learned that sometimes you begin to think about someone, and that such thoughts do not leave you. At first you do not believe it. In the evening you go to Escambron Beach, you watch Miss Draggett, who dances half-naked, half in pajamas, you invite her over to your table, you sit on the naked side. But the next day, from the moment you wake, from the moment you open your eyes, you're still thinking about *that person*. That evening you go to Condado. You gamble a little, you lose, that makes you feel better, but from the roulette table you see the band in its tiny box silhouetted against the sea, the waves surrounding the dance floor, you don't understand that the sea's rhythm frames the human rhythm but you feel your heart stop beating. *That person* is there, and not there. Nelly is there—since we must name names—and she is not. Then you go back to Escambron Beach, you invite Miss Draggett back, but when she comes over to your table, you sit on the pajama side. And then you are furious. You take her to Tartamado's where black women dance. You buy drinks for one named Destinée, she dances naked for you, and then you order champagne, Destinée dances naked with Olivia who is dressed, then Destinée and Olivia, both naked, dance with Evelyn and Marie-Rose of Lima who are dressed. And every day passes that way, switching from the naked half to the dressed half, the way you switch from sun to shade, but without knowing which is sun, which shade. And nothing slakes your thirst for Nelly, nothing erases Nelly's face; nothing except that miserable watercolor in the office of Señor Gomez of the Bull Lines, a watercolor by a French painter Señor Gomez claims is famous and whose name is Erick Alapostole.

"You're looking at my Erick Alapostole, Monsieur Gaston—superb, isn't it?"

The Alapostole is a page in silver tights and a black scarlet-slashed doublet kneeling before a lady in green slippers and a dress cut very low in the back. Of course the back is still there . . . The Alapostole, moreover, is signed and dated 1868. Outside the window you can see the Gien steeple. Gaston had been to Gien. He had been there with Nelly. The page and the queen by Alapostole did not interest him so much as Señor Gomez supposed. But he came over, looked out the window, and he saw Gien. That is what Gaston knew, that this window overlooking Gien consoled him, whereas Miss Draggett, even entirely naked or even entirely dressed—he had tried everything—was a burden to him, and the black ladies were a burden, and the sea was a burden, and the night was a burden . . . By which means ordinary businessmen like Gaston manage to discover that they are in love, successively eliminating all the attractions of the white race and the black, then by the mediation of an Erick Alapostole—it is, really, unthinkable.

Not that Nelly wanted Gaston *not* to love her. On the contrary. With a skill she herself had not suspected, she had hooked Gaston for a long time, for good. With that intuition women always have and men never, she foresaw that her future and Gaston's would overlap. Gaston thought he had secured a year of happiness and freedom with a rich, young, and loving woman. Nelly, who knew she was anything but rich, who knew she would grow old, who knew she didn't love Gaston much, saw the year as a prelude to a life of relative seclusion. Gaston thought he was walking into freedom, especially since Nelly had never used a word, never made a demand that would put him on his guard. Nelly saw clearly that he was walking into an affair, and mentally toward marriage. What Gaston thought was his freedom was Nelly's freedom, which Nelly intended to keep as long as possible. She had done so—she saw Gaston as a captive. But that this captive should think himself on this side of marriage, and in the middle of an affair, whereas the real marriage had taken place and Gaston was on the other side—that was a return Nelly had never imagined. Whereas she was at the stage of sharp words, familiarities, scenes, the satisfactions of an established ménage, here was Gaston wanting to began all over again with what she would never have tolerated from him, even in the past—gentleness, devotion—oh no, impossible, anything but that! What had come over him, telling her not to disturb herself, not to get up, not to go to the kitchen on any excuse, or into her room. Obviously what had come over him was that he wanted to take her in his arms. Not on your life!

It was true. For two months Gaston had thought of nothing but taking Nelly in his arms. Of Nelly's resting her head on his shoulder, of telling her what had happened to him when he saw the Erick Alapostole. (He would make inquiries: if there were any Erick Alapostoles for sale in Paris he would buy one for Nelly. An Alapostole wouldn't be so bad among these Berthe Morisots and these Picassos. It was simpler, but better drawn: in these Picassos, you wouldn't have recognized the Gien steeple.) Of taking Nelly's body in his arms and of saying nothing. When he put out his arms to take the boat, it was Nelly he was taking. When the boat veered east, it was turning Gaston toward Nelly. All the movements of the voyage had been the efforts of men to take Gaston straight to Nelly, a Nelly he would embrace as soon as he saw her and never lose her again, never let her out of his arms. And now, here in this apartment, she was inaccessible. When he sat down, she stood up. When he stood up, she sat down—in places where that infinite embrace was dangerous or absurd: on the little table which could barely hold her, on the glass shelf. But at least she was here, she was in a room fifteen by twenty feet (the height of the ceiling may be omitted), whose doors were closed securely, whose windows overlooked the street from a great height. Even so, there are extraordinary things: to have felt capable of taking this woman with such strength, such skill, and not even to be able to lay a finger on her! It was really a matter of height—she escaped by elevation. It was because the ceiling was so high.

"Where shall we go?"

"Where shall we go?" Going out—when for two months all he had thought of was having this dinner with Nelly, at Nelly's. He had ordered it from Larue. They would send it up. Everything Nelly liked—he would offer it to her, in homage. It was the first thing he had thought of when he landed: feeding Nelly. But that was just what Nelly could not endure, the caresses Gaston would give her by means of the oysters and the wine. Gaston's food.

"Yes, we'll go out. We'll go out—wait a minute."

He dared not speak. He waited a minute. He heard Nelly go into the bathroom, turn on the faucet of the bathtub. He didn't understand. He found Nelly more intimate than before, she was closer than he had imagined, more directly linked to his life. Absence always does that: it gives you intimacy. And at the same time, in another way—he didn't know which, the body's or the mind's—she seemed evasive, inaccessible. Yes, that was it. This return didn't seem like a return, but like a reconciliation between a couple already established and proved, sounded. That was really the worst of it, but that was it. He was returning generous, filled with tenderness, with plans, to this woman who had seen him leave frivolous, selfish. And she granted him a kind of pardon. What would Gaston have thought if he had seen Nelly's preparations for going out. Sitting on a stool beside the tub, she did not move. She let the water run to make Gaston think he couldn't come in. That running water—it was, after all, a stream. Rivers have begun less significantly, and not out of a swan's beak. At least there was a murmur, a flow, a coolness. It was lucky to have found a stream in the house, she would let it flow, she would go back to Gaston when the stream dried up. It was a way of crying she had found here, making this stream flow beside her. Her mother, who criticized her for never crying, could come in now. In a second, more tears had flowed here than her mother had wept in her whole life, including the two enormous ones which had appeared so punctually on her cheeks at her husband's funeral. Poor father. He had found a way of giving her, that day, two more diamonds which had been admired by everyone present.

One day, a day when Gaston would not be here, would no longer be here, Nelly would go sit beside a real stream. One day when Reginald would be here, when Reginald would be, would exist—Reginald, whose existence she no longer understood at this moment. A stream which would not have next to it that hot stream latent in the other faucet, and with some animal coming to drink. Nelly would make no more noise, no more movements than she was making now. And as a matter of fact, stags with twitching tails, frightened does, timorous civets, bold bustards might really have come to drink out of that bathtub, so much did Nelly resemble—more than a woman sitting beside the water—those piped statues out of which a river gushes . . . This pure little stream which after a second's supreme limpidity in Nelly's tub ran directly down the drain . . . Nelly trembled at the thought of its brief career.

She raised her eyes and saw herself in the mirror. For that, a real stream would have been better. Raising her eyes, whether on the bank of the Loire or at the source of the Vienne—she knew, she had been to such places, only not so comfortably, it was always a little marshy—she would have seen the sky. You cannot imagine, if you have not been in the country, how close to the ground the sky comes. The sky was lower than she, near those streams . . . Here in her bathroom she saw herself, and that image, as she was now, mute, motionless, told her more than her own thoughts, insofar as she was thinking. What an exercise for some specialist in hieroglyphics, some scholar to discern which letter, or which word, or which sentence was represented by this young woman sitting oblivious of time, which was dismissed now by the mere injunction of pure water, and by this man coming from the country of pineapples, bananas and seedless grapes to take her in his arms and make her the seed of the world.

It was plain as day. This woman had beside her a

man named Reginald and a man named Gaston. She could have chosen, she could have rid herself of one or the other, if both had had the same density, had lived in the same dimensions. But the one she loved or would love could not materialize himself enough, assume a body heavy enough, have actions and thoughts present enough to count in this everyday life as a being of flesh and blood. Whereas the other one existed, and his presence was a proof of his existence—Reginald's presence was a dream—and Gaston had all the advantages life gives to those who are endowed with it and respect it, despite Nelly's preferences. That, the scholar would have said, that is what is meant by the pretty red inscription on those dimpled lips: a kind of despair. When such an inscription dances, leaps, kisses itself in the mirror, that means it is happy about Gaston's arrival, that it will dine with Gaston, that it will spend the night with Gaston. But if it is fixed, if it nibbles at the corners of the mouth, that means it suddenly resents Reginald for not coming to its rescue, for having stupidly accepted the legend of an inhuman affair without speech, without identity—and for leaving her here, a stubborn, weak woman at grips with someone whose most insignificant tastes and ancestral names she knew as far back as Louis XVIII . . . That is what the scholar would have said, and though Nelly did not understand her reflection that well, she interpreted it just as cruelly.

And already she saw but one remedy, the only remedy there was—that the door must open, that Reginald must come in, that he must explain to Gaston who he was, that he must learn Gaston's real name, his real address, Nelly's real situation and Gaston's too, and that he must discover that Gaston had not been the first, and all the details of Nelly's life must become as familiar to him as to Gaston, including her mother with those two tears, and even things she did not like to remember—her summer in Marly with Luc, her winter in Nice with Hervé, and all this, including Gaston, must leave Reginald smiling, understanding, and Reginald must tell Gaston to leave, and Reginald must stay, and Gaston must go somewhere else to have dinner alone, and Reginald must have dinner here, and Gaston must go to bed alone, and Reginald must go to bed here. My God, what a wonderful day it would be, the day Reginald would use that word, would make a word intimate with his life, his life with Nelly—a word like dinner, a word like bed.

But no Reginald appeared . . . It was late. What was Gaston doing out there in the living room, as if he too had turned on a faucet, turned on the water, or the gas! Gaston had opened a book of poems! That was his faucet. Nelly turned off the water in the tub, abruptly—like a woman who decides not to cry any more. She turned it back on: two drops, just enough to dab some cold water on her eyes. Since Gaston was alive and since Reginald was not, she was certainly going to see.

In five minutes, she abandoned all resemblance to Reginald's mistress—that simple hat, that simple suit.

Her most garish dress, her shiniest pumps, her most arrogant jewels, were on her now. Nelly dressed quickly, harshly, implacably, like a star who is late for her number. It was not difficult to manage—it was Gaston's number.

This number was performed first at Maxim's, where she found Gaston's friends assembled. She ordered all the things she didn't like. After all, she was feeding a body she didn't like. She tried whatever she had always resisted: snails, veal Orloff . . . There was no cutlet Restacheff. Too bad—she detested it. She talked to people at the next table, to people who walked past, to strangers. Gaston wondered why, not suspecting the reason. Nelly was rinsing off the purity Reginald had given her, expurgating a propensity for solitude, for clarity, for untainted words. Gaston did not suspect, nor did she, that she was taking revenge on Reginald. What Nelly thought was her anger against Gaston was a rebellion against Reginald. The Reginald who persisted in not appearing, in not being; whom she would have had to look for in a silent house, a life of hard work, a jumble of naive dreams and terrible lucidity, where Nelly could have no hold over him. Those shrieks she uttered, that plate she threw, that slap she gave—such behavior was everything which might have evoked any other man. If she had deceived Gaston with another man, that other man would be here now.

But Reginald was not here. And he was not in Montmartre. And he was not at Chez Florence. And when Nelly, still as agitated, still as frantic, got back inside the taxi, into which only Gaston got in beside her, that stupid doorman who almost caught her fingers in the car door was not Reginald, and that taxi driver hunched over the wheel—if you suppose he was Reginald, you are wrong: he was a certain Robert Nathan, according to what was typed under the celluloid envelope, and when they reached Nelly's address you might have thought this Robert Nathan would get out, open the taxi door, and turn into Reginald. For stupid women, for impure women, for silly little girls, people named Durand, Piedeveau, Ratisbonne would have turned into a man named Hamlet, Cherubino, Reginald. This one didn't move.

"Move, Reginald! Get out, Reginald!" Nelly exclaimed as she left the taxi.

Gaston made her be still. Moreover, Robert Nathan did not stir. He did not get out. If it was Reginald, he was very cowardly, or very cruel!

They had to walk through the door of the house, a door that opened automatically. No giant named Reginald was leaning against it. Luckily Gaston, who had been drinking, no longer showed that kindness, that ardor which had given his face, before dinner, a certain resemblance to a lovable and loved being. The situation was clearer now. If there were two men so different, there could be two different Nellys. The apartment door upstairs had to be opened with a key: there was not a man leaning against the door inside, not even a little boy named Reginald. A little boy would have been enough: a child Reginald. Nelly would have taken him, she would have put him to bed. In her own bed, of course. He would have been so small in the middle of that big bed, but he would have filled it. She would not have undressed, she would have watched over him. No. There was the bed —opened. What fool had folded back the spread, broached that bed! And Gaston was right there. Nelly escaped.

For an hour, two hours, she spent her time vanishing. She went to the kitchen. The meal Gaston had ordered from Larue was there. She threw it into the garbage, course by course, first the oysters, then the lobster, then the sliced turkey, then the champagne, then the ice, then the cardboard, then the napkins folded into cornucopias by the same fool who had opened the bed. Several days later they came back, by the way, not in cornucopias but in creases, discovered by an honest ragpicker. Then she went into the bathroom, but the water was not the same any more: that afternoon's stream—so pure, so accommodating—no longer flowed. It was an enemy stream now, a terrible stream, a stream ready for anything. Then she opened the pantry door: she would accept anyone who came to her rescue, even up the service stairs. Nelly did not realize that it was an open door, that an open door opens onto the street, onto the night, onto solitude, onto Reginald.

But the maddening thing was to feel that Reginald either did not exist or was not a real man. Obviously he was thinking about her at this moment, but stupidly, childishly, he was thinking about her as a great lady, or a saint, a woman above all contingencies and all discomforts, and here she was alone with her friend back from the West Indies who was coming to propose marriage—without her asking him to, moreover—who was offering her a life, who was offering her everything she wanted before knowing Reginald, and Reginald, his sheet pulled up to his chin—some fool had opened his bed too—was sound asleep at that moment, a stupid smile on his face, and thanking Providence for having granted him a love so distinguished, so tender . . . O my God! what was this incomprehensible notion of duty which told her she had duties toward Gaston, which even filled her with a kind of fraternal pity for Gaston! A contempt for herself which impelled her to sacrifice what she valued more than anything in the world, herself. O my God! Let someone come through the pantry door, if not Reginald, at least a specialist in consciences, one of those men who claim to understand the human heart and take advantage of the fact to write about it, a man who would have seen what was happening now, someone like Paul Bourget—he had just died—his work would be cut out for him, a kind of secular confessor who would tell her what to do. She would obey, she promised, whatever he said; she gave him full authority, she gave authority to philosophy, to ethics, to psychology! It would have been so good to see such a man climbing her service staircase, a man in a frock coat with a decoration in his buttonhole.

"Here," she would have called softly. "Here, Bourget! You're needed here. Quick!"

Thus Nelly used up every possible means. Gaston

did not call her. There was only one hope left. Her one hope was if, there in that bedroom, she suddenly found not Gaston but Reginald. No, from that cough, she recognized him—it was Gaston, all right. Then what did this silence mean? Was it sleep, or fear of making a noise, or a decision to be tender? That would be dreadful, since the two Nellys were so clearly separated, since none of the qualities of one Nelly overlapped the other, since they knew nothing about each other, it would be dreadful if the man to whom the harsh, conscious, selfish Nelly was promised gave what was intended for the other one.

She could reassure herself. Nothing of the kind occurred.

5

Nelly was honest or at least open with herself. She wanted to find out if she was playing aboveboard, if that part of her which in the last few months had appeared to be so different from the rest, that gentle, divested part, ready for devotion and poverty, was a lie invented to justify her affair with Reginald in her own eyes. She had not seen Reginald again, she had not written to him. Sometimes she almost hoped that nothing further would be heard from that quarter, that Reginald was really incapable of making himself real. If he would not take shape, he would have to take the consequences.

It was silly, still hoping to find him there when she came home in the evening, or when she ran to the telephone. Whatever stone life turned during the week, the month, Gaston was under it; shifting a piece of furniture, moving a minute, immediately revealed Gaston. Nowhere Reginald. Of course if she forced her way into his apartment, if she went to his lectures, waited in front of his door until he came out . . . But a kind of protocol around their liaison forbade such practices, an inviolable protocol. Nor was Reginald the kind of man you met in the street, or during intermission. It was a pity, right here in Paris, to suffer such anguish of departure and inequality, worse than any inequality of race—the kind suffered by a geisha or a nautch girl when the naval officer vanishes.

With that aspect of eternity, of supreme permanence, what else had Reginald been, after all, but a superlative naval officer or aviator in Nelly's heart? Why hadn't he been a real ensign! But that nameless ship of which he was the helmsman, that special firmament which directed him—in the long run it became intolerable. Nelly felt it, going to bed at night, waking in the morning, she felt it: here was a wonderful opportunity to unite the two Nellys in a single person. It was up to Reginald: the futile Nelly could have been absorbed by the other one, along with all her coquetry and lustre; Nelly was amazed to see a kind of softness permeating her most habitual actions. She had taken the initiative. She had written Reginald she was going away, she had even given the train schedule. She had even gone to the station. But Reginald had not come. Since then, Nelly had not concealed herself. She went to the races, to lectures, to concerts. You couldn't help seeing her in the Rue de la Paix, in restaurants. She was on parade, noisy, volatile, overflowing. She compromised herself. Everyone saw her, heard her, except for Reginald.

Sometimes, in Montmartre or at the Feria, she hoped he would be there to see how his ideal mistress shouted with the musicians or danced with unknown partners; she would have liked going even further, making Reginald believe she was a wicked woman, inflicting scandal upon his soul. Gaston wondered why Nelly let a hideous and famous banker take such liberties, then broke her champagne glass over his head—it was a little genre scene she was offering Reginald. A madness accompanied, moreover, by the absolute impossibility of reaching her, of touching her . . . Poor Gaston was mystified.

Around five in the morning, the night of his arrival, he got up, dressed quietly in order not to waken Nelly. She was fast asleep, but suddenly, as he was leaving, Gaston had glanced in the mirror and seen her eyes wide open, staring at him. They were dry, clear eyes, eyes which had obviously not slept all night. It was less a stare than the glare of a beast of prey. Then the eyes had closed again, and when Gaston returned on tiptoe to the bedside, he had not dared speak a word or touch this woman sleep had turned into a statue. He had never referred to the incident. There was only one explanation for that stare, Gaston couldn't be mistaken about it—he had seen that stare in the eyes of Nelly's first fiancé when he had taken her away from him: hatred. That the man you take a woman away from should transfer his hatred to the eyes of the woman who lets herself be taken—that was no explanation. Gaston was a great specialist in accounting, and his deductions had won him a high place in the alimentary councils of the world. He thought only by paragraphing and subdividing his ideas. But then he thought. Either that stare was the special hatred of an instant, or it was the expression of a constant hatred. In the first hypothesis, either it was the anger provoked by that agitated night and his brutality, or else the end of a dream. In the first case of this first hypothesis, Nelly was right, and her hatred would be ephemeral, especially if he returned to his project of being a friend, a mild and indulgent husband. The second case also subdivided into two solutions: either she had dreamed of men, of a brutal man, and it was natural that her eyelids, opening, should reveal that vindictive nocturnal gaze. Or else she had dreamed of him, of a brutal Gaston. And such hatred, as a matter of fact, was explicable. And he would arrange for it to pass. The second hypothesis, of a constant hatred, was harder for Gaston to understand. Either the stare represented a generalized hatred for all men: which he could not hold against her, for such accesses of hatred were frequent among women and justified too, for men deserved no better. Or else it was Nelly's individual hatred for him, Gaston, but then he did not quite understand, for he had just offered her everything he possessed, his life, his name, his fortune. Perhaps, in fact, he had been in too much of a hurry. Perhaps Nelly loved him for himself, wanted to love him freely, unconditionally—all great souls are like that. Still, the fact was that poor Gaston had reached these two conclusions in any case: Nelly was not wrong and had to be won over by tenderness. It was precisely these prospects which had provoked Nelly's stare.

A stare which now, for Gaston, eclipsed all Nelly's other expressions. Ever since that night, Nelly's eyes, when he observed them, seemed mute, seemed blind. Sometimes he wanted to see them just as they had been that night—at least that would be the end of a dream, a dream in which every man in the world had insulted Nelly, in which she had seen men do to women what they habitually do: humiliate them, flout them, deceive them, violate them, kill them. The day Gaston himself dreamed that someone had taken Nelly away from him, he must have had eyes like that!

He provoked those eyes. He forced himself to be caustic, harsh, to make Nelly open eyes which would seem *somewhere else,* as if they had suddenly appeared on her breast, on the nape of her neck, and Gaston did not suspect that in his invented harshness, his assumed vulgarity, instead of provoking Nelly, he was soothing her, and that because of his bad manners those eyes, instead of appearing on Nelly's forehead, or her chin, gently reappeared in their habitual sockets . . .

*

*   *

There was something else in Nelly's eyes. There were those preposterous memories of Reginald which invaded her at the most unexpected moments. A hat the wind had blown away during a walk, a sock she had thrown out Reginald's window and which had caught on the branches of a tree. Two memories to resuscitate a passion—it was little enough.

But it was enough. A hat and a sock—it would have been an old sock, if it survived so well it was because the twigs must have poked through the stitches—replaced all the special instruments of love which other lovers require: Wagner, jealousy, or journeys. The hat and the sock provoked all the impulses of tenderness or devotion just as infallibly, and by their very modesty as auxiliaries gave love a simplicity and a pathos worthy of a convent, a prison. Nor would Nelly and Reginald ever weary of these humble episodes: a day would come when this hat would grow old, would no longer leap up, when the hunt for it would be replaced by memories of its disappearance, and also when it would be replaced by another hat, and that one by still another. As for the sock, you couldn't be sure after its resistance to the May tornado, but for many years in any case, what unquestioned happiness, what assured discussions of the volatile destiny of hates and the immortality of socks! And with Reginald, all that was enough. It was even too much. If he had come bareheaded, or if the tree had been virgin of its bizarre fruit, a single remark would have played the part in Nelly's life which hitherto the most extraordinary events or memories had been unable to play.

For two hours, for three, Nelly suffered, for who would claim that even humble allies can keep you from suffering. There are hats on the heads of men in the street, there are hats left on chairs in hallways, almost identical to the real hat sometimes—the initials are different. There are socks in the shop windows, some of them absurd, and even more so caught on an acacia in a Parisian courtyard. And sometimes you find one, on a rainy day, a black one, the same faded black, soiled by the street, flattened into a corner of the gutter, and so much like the real one—no initials to check—that you wonder if it isn't the one, if a special wind hasn't blown down the Boulevard Pereire and across the Place Clichy, and over the trains of the Gare Saint-Lazare, and above the Opera, bringing it right to the couturier's door. And besides, all this was too much, all this presupposed sight, words, whereas Nelly blind, deaf, and mute would have known an incredible happiness with a blind, deaf, and mute Reginald. Voice, eyes, ears had been necessary for them to meet, not for them to know each other . . . Nelly no longer doubted it: it must have been because they did not know each other, because all their senses (aside from the one plants have) were unemployed, that they had enjoyed such incredible absence of the world, such unreality, such happiness. On the Champs-Elysées, behind Chez Laurent, there is a black rag dangling from the top of a plane tree. No gardener's eye has spotted it yet. Nelly sometimes made detours to see if it was still there.

"What are you looking at up there?" Gaston asked.

"Am I looking up?"

"There's nothing wrong with looking up."

The main thing was to keep Gaston from seeing the rag. If she denied it, he would stop and look. "I was trying to see if there were any nests. But there wouldn't be, so high."

"That depends," Gaston said. "If it's going to be a cool summer, the nests are high. And low when the summer's hot—the birds build them in the shade then. But what are you looking at up there? You were looking way up."

"No." And suddenly she understood. Perhaps because Gaston was there. The presence of a human being always provides a way of deciphering your own life. The fact that he loves you allows you to imagine how he can be disappointed, by what he can be humiliated, so that you guess right and take advantage of it for yourself. What could humble this poor trusting creature, what could make him absurd, what could deride his devotion, his suddenly ennobled love? If there was something, surely life, as we all know life, had imagined and realized it!

All she had to do was find it to be sure it was possible. What could baffle this fiancé sitting in his car beside his future wife, this confident suitor who had found, only this morning, an entirely satisfactory explanation for last night's stare, who after years of vulgar and complacent existence, was groping toward nobility and purity—what was it? Of course! Suppose that in five minutes this fiancée he thought was so faithful and friendly was in a lover's arms, her mouth pressed to a lover's mouth, in five minutes or in ten;

and suppose she deceived him in her body and soul and in her future life to the end of time and the consummation of the Last Judgment! There was no doubt about it, if that was it, then this ignoble life had prepared everything so that it could be arranged.

Suddenly Nelly was positive that in ten minutes she could be in Reginald's arms. She had felt for several hours now that everything was being prepared to degrade this candid creature who went on telling her about nests in trees, everything in Nelly known as demons, lust, the flesh, everything in Reginald known as archangels, fidelity to a beloved image, disinterestedness, so that by this collaboration of supreme evil and supreme good, with the assistance of fast taxis, Nelly was positive—she had never before been positive, she was young—that here on earth, every great infamy is always admirably ready, admirably prepared, in the same hypocrisy, by the accursed powers and the blessed powers, and in the present case, that love had marvelously conjugated everything to demean love. Reginald's pure love on the one side, Gaston's marvelous love on the other.

Of course, thanks to Nelly, there could be some fine additional ignominies, thanks to Nelly, thanks to the absurd circumstances that there was only one Nelly and two of them, or rather that there were two Nellys but that she had only one face, only one mouth. How much God must have regretted inventing Time, which permitted deception only in succession and alternation! He would certainly do better in the next Creation!

Yes, that was it. In five minutes, she didn't know how, but the best means and the best pimp was surely the demiurge, she would be lying beside Reginald. And to settle any possible doubt, pity was involved—she took pity on Gaston! As the rain inevitably falls on the little boy in his new sailor suit, Nelly's pity fell on Gaston. It streamed over that envelope of a future husband, credulous, kind, honorable man. She would have to put a stop to it. Gaston was taking her to look at an eighteenth-century painting in an antique shop. Very pretty. A woman bathing. The painter had put in the refraction of her legs in the water. Very curious. Gaston was eager to know what Nelly thought of the refraction . . . Suddenly she stopped him.

"Oh, my poor Gaston! I have to go home, right now, right this minute!"

"Right this minute?"

"I have to change before I go to Mother's."

*

* *

In the car, Gaston asked question after question. He forced Nelly to swear on her father's head.

And Nelly's dead father answered Gaston's demand: "Swear you never lived with Paul H."

"Go on, swear it—you see, I'm satisfied if you say just the initial, the first letter is one word less for the lips of a dead father. It's the one thing I want to spare you—swear it, my love, my daughter, swear it. Perjure yourself on my head. It's not a living head, cut off at the neck, the kind that will open its eyes at your perjury, that will utter a cry in the grave. This is a head without lips. The earth fills its mouth—it won't answer you. The earth fills its ears—it won't hear you. Swear: not on that smile you loved but on those teeth your mother loathed, on those eyebrows she thought were too thick when by accident—what else could I do?—those nights I had crept into her bed, softly and without permission, I sometimes had to rest my head somewhere . . . All that's left of my head is what she had no use for—the brows, the jaws. Swear on them, my living daughter. With your lips, with your brain that fills the lovely curve of your forehead so neatly, with your little mind that I love so dearly, swear on my empty skull, on my missing eyes . . ."

And Nelly had sworn! And Gaston, understanding Nelly's distress at this obstacle with all the instinct of jealousy, had gradually brought her to an imperceptible perjury on the head of her dead father, up to the day he himself had doubted. And Nelly—for women have such a need of help, of room in their hearts for truth—Nelly had been led to look for it elsewhere, and had found it in her son. Along with this father who permitted her soul such lies, who helped her lie, she wanted a son who would not permit them. When would that son appear? Where would he come from? It didn't matter. Maybe he would be the son existed within her, pure, impregnable, luminous. She of this very Gaston she had to lie to. But he already was carrying a square diamond who was her son. She was glad that he didn't move, that he didn't yet exist. Of course some day he would have to exist, but once he existed he would begin to be less hers. How she regretted having revealed him to Gaston one day, one day when Gaston had accused her of letting Hervé kiss her, and when, outraged, she had sworn on her son that nothing of the kind had occurred. Wretched Hervé, who had forced her to reveal her weakness to Gaston! In vain she had tried to make him suppose she adored Helene Guise and that it was painful to swear on Helene Guise's head. She had managed a few good lies on Helene's charming head, but there was something so frivolous, so giddy about it that soon Gaston could no longer take it seriously as an altar of truth. The day after the day Nelly had sworn on Helene's head that she would not go to the swimming pool and he had run into her there, Helene's head was pinker and prettier than ever. Falsehood made Helene's head flourish, whereas Nelly felt it inflicted a kind of extra death on that poor paternal head which had nonetheless consented to all her lies.

She got out of the car, outraged. "What does my son have to do with my mother? Believe me if you want to. I won't swear on anything—even on your own head."

"You won't swear on anything because you don't want to swear on your son's head."

"You don't believe me?"

She seemed outraged. Gaston, with his mania for deductions, tried to work it out for himself. Either she was outraged because she was telling the truth. Or because she was telling a lie. In the second case, her outrage was so extreme that it must be a big lie, a lie which covered others. In the first case, it was merely the splendid outrage of an innocent woman, the kind of outrage that indicated her candor was limitless, stubborn and indomitable. That was how Gaston thought of Nelly—a kind of wayward, stubborn nymph, but of indomitable candor. That was what Nelly was like! "I believe you," he said.

He said. Which didn't keep him from parking the car out of sight in the next street and coming back to keep an eye on her door. He came back just in time to see Nelly—a little black coat open over her bright dress—run out the door and jump into a taxi which took her in the wrong direction if she was going to her mother's. Two possibilities, of course. Either Nelly had deliberately lied to him. Or else she had told the truth. Either she was dishonest and had occupations in her life which did not concern Gaston—a vice, a lover. Or else it was her mother's fault, her mother had forgotten that Nelly was coming because of her absentmindedness, or her selfishness, or her affair with that bearded man. Between the two hypotheses, Gaston naturally did not hesitate one second. Of course it was typical of Nelly's mother not to have left her a minute to change her clothes. One puts on a black coat over a red dress only to rush off in answer to the absurd summons of a mother or a family.

And suddenly Gaston trembled. An idea had occurred to him which filled him with sadness, with pity, and with love. That son to whom Nelly alluded as if he were a future son, at whose name she started—perhaps he really existed! That joy and ferocity she revealed at the mere mention of his name—perhaps it could be explained by the fact that there was a real child, living with some foster mother in Vincennes or the Champ-de-Mars, a baby who was Nelly's own. Perhaps Nelly was rushing off like that, in her ill-matching clothes, to Nelly's son, alerted by telephone to an attack of measles or appendicitis . . .

Of course! That was it. Nelly's face never lied. Only maternal love wore that mask of tenderness and obstinacy. She was rushing to her son.

*

*   *

She had been right. When you trust to fate as to the worst pimp of all, you are always right. The law by which women deceive their husband on just the day that husband is noble and good, when he is killed in battle, if it is wartime, by which sons die at just the moment when the father is clowning at his old school banquet—the law could do no less in the present case. Gaston was beginning to have a noble soul, which had its price. Its price today was as follows: this woman who was frivolous, selfish, unconcerned when she would be his wife, was in tears on her way to meet another man.

She was in tears, but not sobs. In the dim room, Reginald would have known nothing if his hands hadn't been wet. There were tears around Nelly. He held her in his arms without giving her time to take off her black coat, and she was glad he did. For that way Reginald could not see her red dress. She had the impression that this red dress, which she hadn't taken the time to replace by a dark one, might betray her. Red was her other life, like jade, like magenta. If he saw this red dress, Reginald would see the flaw in her life. Reginald might guess . . . That red dress knew Gaston, Gaston in a tuxedo, Gaston naked, Gaston standing, Gaston lying down. Nelly had the impression that if Reginald took off her coat, a kind of flaying would occur. Providence was not likely to be more considerate of Reginald than of Gaston. This moment of wonderful affection—Reginald would pay for it by naiveté, by an incomprehension of the situation which touched on naiveté. It was Reginald who held Nelly's coat against her dress, over her dress. Usually the first thing he did was to help her out of her coat, to rid Nelly of that first lie which was her modest appearance, then of the second lie which was her dark dress, so that without running the risk of touching the truth he arrived at that supreme lie which was Nelly's body, the only lie she could really be sure of, for objects betray you so unexpectedly. He examined, he caressed these garments from which Nelly had removed the dressmaker's labels, the laundry marks, and whose anonymity she had checked before coming to meet Reginald, like the woman who wants to commit suicide incognito.

But today, when he had only to part the coat to see Nelly's true colors, Reginald turned up its collar, he buttoned its buttons, as if her tears were the result of a terrible chill. Nelly was ready to succumb, to tell the truth; wearing that red dress in broad daylight, she would no longer have the strength to lie—she had the feeling the dress confessed everything for her. And in her anxiety, she admired that cynical hypocrisy of fate, which as soon as you abandon your lie takes it over and continues on its own. She was nothing but truth at that moment, she was nothing more than Nelly; body and soul had abandoned the role she had played for Reginald for three months, she asked only to be free of a deception which was becoming impossible, even if disaster was the result.

But on that momentarily authentic body, fate pasted a lie, and with Reginald's own hands, so that gradually Nelly came to herself, in other words to her duplicity; Nelly realized it was growing dark, that she had only a few more minutes to wait in Reginald's arms to assure that illusory present by which their love survived. She made him sit down, sat down on his lap. He embraced her. He thought he was embracing the one human truth: a love terrified by happiness, by calm, by certainty. He was embracing a human, indeed a female form which, in her lover's arms as though deep in the safest burrow, passed in silence from truth to deception, peering into the shadows, waiting until they were thick enough to dissolve into them, and who as soon as she saw her lover blind twice over—by darkness, by devotion—was naked in one second. One second or two, time enough for a woman to change truths. With an extra second to roll the red dress into a shapeless mass and conceal it in a pile of laundry. You never can tell.

"My love, light of my life," he said.

6

Sometimes it seemed to Nelly that Reginald's inability to suspect the truth was no more than a nobility which enslaved her, which sanctified that two-hour part she played every day, which made their meeting, for her, a kind of revenge on the shames and stupidities of life. They were the vows she took before meeting him. Each additional lie seemed a way of getting farther from reality, an additional truth in this fictive world.

On more than one occasion, unable to sustain such marvelous hours by telling the truth, Nelly had been obliged to invent a little sister who had died, and a favorite pet, and running away from home by night as a girl. She had had only brothers, had had no fondness even for a cat, and had always been afraid of the dark; but in order to obey that inspiration which ordered her to resemble the Nelly whom Reginald loved, a ravishing sister had appeared, and a doe, and a nocturnal adventure, suitcase in hand.

It was the suitcase that had given her away. She had opened it in the woods, and out fell the objects that had put her pursuers on the track. Reginald listened, charmed by everything, believing everything. She knew her lies could not remain where they had started or they would be discovered immediately: they would have to bloom, to spread. Sometimes, when her improvisations were most extravagant, she had felt a kind of well-being, an ecstasy which she unwittingly achieved because she had attained a kind of truth, the truth of poetry. But sometimes Reginald's credulity annoyed her. She felt something like pity for him, accompanied by contempt. That this prodigy of psychological penetration, who saw into the very heart of Venizelos or Stalin, did not realize, did not even suspect that the woman in his arms was not an extraordinary Austro-French orphan who had remained pure in marriage, but a wretched little creature burdened with an affair and the most bourgeois of families—that sometimes robbed Nelly of her admiration for Reginald, and there were times when she was tempted to make him into her plaything.

There were times when her lies were intended not only to adorn Nelly for their magnificent ceremonies, but to abase Reginald in relation to her. Not that she loved him any the less. But if only she could be free of a certain threat, the burdensome threat of what was high, pure, unsullied—lying was her revenge on that threat. In spite of everything, her lies defiled Reginald. The fact that he was living in a false atmosphere, that a woman he loved had just lied to him, was neither a halo nor a purification. To accept lies that way, without its even occurring to him to question them, was to be compromised. The problem was that her lies to Reginald were not the same as her lies to Gaston. The lies to Gaston, she felt, could go on forever. She would never be satisfied with them—there would always be a third person she would have to conceal from Gaston. But with Reginald, her lie had to be a special one, for she would never again find a Reginald. No man would ever again ask her to rise above herself, would ever consider her a perfection of chastity, a miracle of truth. So that she felt there was no other means of approaching Reginald.

Sometimes she wondered if Reginald himself was playing a game, if he knew all along what was happening. She laid traps for him. Perhaps the Reginald who seemed so remote, so lofty, was merely selfish, merely greedy, so satisfied by an affair without murmurs, without munificence, that he decked it out as a marvel in order not to deck it out with gold and diamonds. She wondered if she shouldn't treat him like any other man, like Gaston, if she shouldn't think of marrying Reginald, of choosing between Reginald and Gaston. Despite his desire to see the affair as miraculous, wasn't it just an affair like any other? If Reginald accepted this silence, this dissimulation of their love, perhaps it was simply because he had a jealous mistress, or because he didn't want Nelly involved in the rest of his life. It was so easy to invent imaginary palaces in which to lodge your mistress when you didn't want her inside your apartment. So that sometimes the two affairs came to seem the same, and sometimes the question arose for Nelly that arises not for the woman who must choose between an extraordinary life and an ordinary one, but for the woman who must choose between two lovers: which one did she really love, which one did she want to live with?

But that was just the trouble: as soon as she asked this question, she realized she loved Reginald more than Gaston, and the value of this love as it had grown, however disguised, intimidated Nelly so much she dared not approach it. The question then became quite different: could Nelly be all day long the gentle and perfect woman she managed to be for two hours? Could she extinguish that life of coquetry, of selfishness, of temper and triviality which she lived for the other twenty-two? Sometimes, in Reginald's arms, she was sure she could. She felt that just a quarter of an hour would be enough, or some morning when Reginald was asleep and she could go over the bills with their servants, or make phone calls while Reginald was working—time enough to be that other Nelly again, the one who was a little greedy, a little argumentative, and then be free to be Reginald's Nelly the rest of the day . . .

No, as far as she was concerned, it could all work out. There was poor Gaston to get rid of, that would be hard, but it's an exaggeration to suppose you can't bear the sufferings of someone you don't love. Actually, it was about Reginald that she had her doubts. An ordinary woman has no equal when it comes to analyzing a man of genius. Perhaps what Reginald liked about those two hours was their singularity. Perhaps the delicious elevation of those two hours resulted in his conviction that they had been wrested from an opposing life, contrary to the laws, the rites of love, even though they were merely a rendezvous like fifty thousand others which occur in Paris at the same hour. Reginald's solicitude for a woman whom he believed not only faithful but intact, not only free but rich, not only delicate but cultivated—would it not turn sour once he knew her? Did he love Nelly, or did he love the woman he thought she was? How harshly he spoke of women like Nelly, women who are deceptive, selfish, women who have two lovers.

Since Reginald insisted on just one Nelly, there was just one way for her to be happy with him, which was never to evoke other Reginalds. To have absolutely no contact with anything in that perfect life, which would otherwise become intolerable. The light, the truth in this particular case could lead only to duplicity, shadows and suffering. Sometimes, of course, such happiness lacked something: a future. Since neither Reginald nor Nelly ever mentioned the past, it followed that they could not mention the future either. The future is inhabited by railroad stations, hotels, landscapes with good restaurants or Romanesque churches which ineluctably connect, even if you change companions, with the hotels, the railroad stations, the meals or admirations of the past. Reginald had never yet said: "Some day we'll do this, next winter we'll go there . . ."

Without summer, without autumn, all seasons reckoned only by the leaves on the tree around the suspended sock, Nelly's daily entrance into Reginald's apartment resembled an entrance into what lacks all future and all hope: Eternity. Like a lamb that has fallen into a well, Nelly realized that the sky over her life was higher and lovelier, but she could no longer stir. She would have given anything if only Reginald would speak of that future! Then she could be free of everything! But by persisting in that alarming or merely stupid silence of his, it was as if Reginald's love were already determined—with other habits, with another woman—for a date which would come one day, and as if her own future were Gaston.

Poor Gaston! He didn't make life any easier either. Had he not convinced himself, by the passion with which Nelly refused to swear on her son's head, that Nelly actually had one—had a son! He now explained all Nelly's behavior by this non-existent child. If he decided she was evasive or irritable, that couldn't be in her nature—Gaston was positive this evasive, irritable woman could be constant and tender—tenderer than all the rest. If she wasn't, there were only two explanations, the first and the second. The first was that she didn't love Gaston. That was inconceivable. If Nelly didn't love Gaston, all she had to do was say so, and he would vanish. If she spent three-quarters of the day with him, and every Sunday, it was because she did love him. If she seemed glad to marry him, it was because she loved him. If she sometimes spent the night with him, it was because she loved him.

Of course, there remained the man Gaston referred to as the Efficient Cause. What a base creature! Yet he made Nelly seem all the nobler—her reticence toward Gaston was only her distress at not yet being able to tell him her secret. Those impatient gestures were only the shame of owing a son to a seducer. Moreover, a seducer who would someday have to deal with Gaston. That dark dress in which she left every afternoon around four—for Gaston had noticed that too—was the classic dress in which guilty mothers went to visit their sons.

At last, after several weeks of profound suffering, Gaston had not only grown accustomed to this son, but asked for nothing better than to love him. He no longer doubted the boy's existence. Twenty times he had tried to trap Nelly: she had never answered as if she were childless. If he discussed a trip, or jewels, or food, there was always a son's presence behind her answer. Nelly didn't want to go to Java with him: even a woman who had loved another man would have been happy to go to Java . . . Nelly seemed not to care about jewels any more, even the square diamond: as Cornelia had proved, for a woman there is one jewel more precious than a square diamond, and only one—a son . . . Nelly had less appetite for the highly spiced dinners they used to eat: some racial memories warn women who have a child not to spoil their milk by food that is too highly spiced; even when they are no longer nursing, the premonition lingers . . . Gaston even knew the son's name: Reginald. One day he had found it in Nelly's engagement book: "Don't forget Reginald's birthday April 15." The English name had troubled him: the father might be English, but if Nelly had given the boy an English name as well, it was because she still had some feeling for her seducer. After all, if she had had none, that would scarcely have done her credit! Thus Gaston, who believed he loved Nelly because she was a virgin, alone, and loved only him, gradually consented to the fact that Nelly had been seduced, that she had loved another man . . . The important thing was that Nelly must not suspect his suspicions, until the day his love and his tenderness would make her tell him the whole story.

But Gaston's discretion was of a rather crude quality. It consisted in never lingering at Nelly's when she went out in her dark clothes. With a reticence which awakened Nelly's suspicions, he no longer asked questions at that time of day but kissed her hand, respectfully, gave her a knowing smile, and left. He even asked if she didn't have something she might want to do by herself on Sunday afternoon; he would go to the races. This so startled Nelly that she let several days go by without seeing Reginald. She decided Gaston was following her. She had Helene Guise keep an eye on him: far from following her, Gaston had returned to his office. He took an immense delight in working now, in creating new deals while Nelly was with her son. From five to seven, while she was playing with her little Reginald—what a pity he couldn't give the boy a present on April 15!—Gaston felt inspired, he found new openings for corn, rice, and sugar—new futures. Tea had an unsuspected future! It was through Helene that Nelly found out. Helene wasn't sure, but she had the impression that Gaston knew Nelly had some other occupation in her life besides loving Gaston, but that this knowledge only made him all the happier now, stronger than ever . . . Helene thought that Gaston thought that Nelly had a child living with a foster mother somewhere. She was talking about it when Gaston came in.

There was no doubt about it. He thought something of the kind. Which explained his reticence, his moderation these last few weeks. It was because he respected a young mother. Nelly may not have been clever enough, but she was cruel enough to savor the ironies of existence. That this fool was making up ways to give her free time, that he was providing her this innocent alibi, was really too much. Those almost reverent farewells at around four-thirty, that insistence with which he asked Helene to the races—it was all intolerable and absurd.

My God, how hard men make life for you—as much by their kindness as by their cruelty, by their generosity as by their selfishness! The complications of their small-mindedness are quite enough without the complications of their broad-mindedness as well! The game that had been so easy to play with a dull and insensitive Gaston she would now have to play with a tolerant and sentimental . . . partner! She would no longer have to conceal merely love now, merely the life and death of her soul, the flames and tears of joy, a sated and ecstatic body—all of which, with a well-timed headache, was easy enough, and a screen of Nelly's quality would not have let a glimmer of light or heat reach Gaston. But now she would have to appeal for help all day long to that son who occurred to her only during a few lies, a few promises, she would have to deceive that son, flout that son by dealing with him in this lamentable fashion. If Gaston had only decided she was busy with a nephew, with a retarded child, with the deaf-and-dumb of this world! She would have linked one of these to Reginald, she would have found a way to make Gaston's imaginings into a truth!

Men believe in the truth only when it takes after the model they devise for it—so much the worse if it is made after the fact, if it is posterior to events. What they really care about is the justification of illusion or lies. But Nelly, who was quite confident about existent beings, was not at all confident about non-existent ones. To turn herself into a mother for Gaston, into a virgin for Reginald, would have afforded her no difficulty at all—neither spiritual nor physical. But this son who didn't exist embarrassed her, shamed her. The imagination and the future should be free of lies. Nelly felt quite at ease in the labyrinth of her words, in the lies of her daily life. But she didn't want to lie in her unlived life. She decided to do nothing to convince Gaston she had a son. No matter how it turned out. You have to lie with what is at hand, otherwise it is really lying. She would try to make Gaston believe she smoked opium. It would be easy to make him run into her some day with a Chinese. Helene knew the Persian *chargé d'affaires,* who was very thick with the Japanese secretary. As for the other one, the imaginary son, that monster Reginald who was trying to cheat her out of a future she would not renounce on any pretext, he too would see.

Reginald saw, as a matter of fact . . . but not at all what Nelly thought she was letting him see. There really is a difference between an intelligent man and a man who is not: the difference is that an intelligent man, even when he doesn't guess, breaks nothing, destroys nothing, circulates among the soul's most fragile furniture like a cat among crystal goblets. Reginald, who knew nothing and guessed nothing, never said a word, never made a gesture which could be the word or gesture of an ignorant man. Everything about him assumed—whether it was his way of greeting Nelly when she came in, of kissing her, of making her sit down beside him, of talking, not about their love for each other but about wild animals, about three-toed sloths and snow leopards—that he knew perfectly well that women's lives are difficult, that they may have sons, that they may not have them, and that the world, that delicious place, is merely a sordid and ignoble inn. And without suspecting the threat, Reginald dispelled it forever, he spoke about their love, about that love he refused to locate, to materialize.

7

Neither a chance encounter nor an anonymous letter alerted Reginald. Nor did he arrive at the truth by those arguments *ab absurdo* which mathematicians employ to discover the true identity of a triangle. There simply formed, above his happiness, the eddies which form above any happiness won over fate, against fate. Reginald and Nelly owed their happiness to each other, they had made it with their own hands, apart from the distractions of Paris, and they were proud of it; their pride did not parade itself, but swelled with power in the face of others' miserable happiness. So there occurred to Reginald what happens to the parvenus of happiness and to the proud, in other words what occurred to Oedipus, or to Gyges . . . In his vanity and his satisfaction, he was the sole artisan of a revelation which fate might have disdained, judging it insufficiently exalted.

What revelation, Reginald asked himself one day,

on his way to meet Nelly, would cause him most surprise and pain: the discovery, he answered, that this incredible delight was a delusion, that he was deceived, that Nelly was a liar. The very notion made him laugh. It was summer now. All the flowers in the Bois were in bloom, they filled the air with their fragrance. The Arc de Triomphe, attacked from one side by the sun, was attacked from all sides by a kind of grandeur and a calcareous felicity. And Reginald felt that his happiness was of the same quality as the roses and the monument, and he knew that these roses lived on rotten earth, and that this Arc de Triomphe was built on death, as both Villon and Joseph Prudhomme told him on that spiritual afternoon. Of course he did not intend to take the analogy any further. But in that same game which seduced the happy Oedipus the day he asked himself: Suppose my wife were my mother, and that old fool I rode down were my beloved father, and my daughter my sister, and my father my uncle . . . , Reginald was asking himself: Suppose this explosion of purity, truth and devotion which is our love were a mixture of hypocrisy, venality and concubinage, suppose Nelly's lovely mouth belonged to any number of men, suppose Nelly's tongue, which produces against her palate and her teeth only sounds as true as a tuning fork's, mingled at its tip both ruses and lies, suppose Nelly's hand . . . In short, everything that was supremely unimaginable, impossible . . . In short, the truth.

He was still laughing when, at the end of the

afternoon, Nelly still in his arms, he said: "You know, Nelly, I know everything."

"Oh?"

"Since yesterday, I've known everything."

"Good," Nelly replied. She had dozed off. She was motionless. Her eyes were closed; for a moment everything was closed within and around her. She found herself in the dark den of her own existence, where she didn't like to take refuge. But she needed that refuge, even if only for a minute. Not that she believed Reginald knew anything. If he had suspected the least crumb of reality, he would not have been, during these two hours, what he had just been, the same Reginald as yesterday, and as the day before yesterday. But she heard that "I know everything" as a knock at the door by whatever it is which pursues those who live on mirages or on lies or on one of those occasionally indispensable conventions known as myths. It was Reginald who was knocking. He had knocked by accident. But Nelly felt that it was not an accident, that there was a threat in the air. Of course she would not answer that knock. The wind shakes the door through which the thief will enter. But you cannot be too careful. As though intoxicated by sleep, she turned over, stretched, shook off the dust of truth which had suddenly fallen on her arms, her face, and turning away her eyes, her breast, her belly, her knees —every surface which had betrayed and through which betrayal would someday come, left to Reginald's gaze only her shoulders, her back, her waist—whatever part of herself she was sure of, and in a sudden fatigue which was an excuse, the only excuse today, abandoned herself to sleep.

Reginald gazed at her. She was detached from him. Never had she detached herself that way—so abruptly, so completely. Suddenly, and for the first time, she gave herself up in his bed to a solitary slumber. Instead of clinging to him, struggling to hold onto him against approaching sleep, it was as if she had suddenly yielded, had suddenly abandoned everything, had given herself to something stronger than sleep, something to do with oblivion, with nothingness. As a matter of fact, Nelly was alone; for the first time Reginald saw her alone. Her entire attitude, her entire body were those of an existence in which there was no Reginald. He saw as much of Nelly as you see of the person who leads you among the dead: the back—a back which did not recognize him, with which he had nothing to do, something as unknown to him and as little concerned with him as Nelly's past could be, a featureless personage who owed nothing to their love. He saw her suddenly dimmed, without that scintillation of their passion, he saw for the first time what Nelly was without love. His heart stopped. For next to that lustreless Nelly he saw their love detached from her and from them both—like luggage you could collect or abandon for good. Their love no longer appeared to Reginald as a part of themselves, as a mixture of themselves: it was there, in the room, it was still there, but as a third person whom you can, if you like or if you must, abandon.

Yet it was great, that love. Indeed, detached that way, it seemed even greater, more powerful, more commanding: but it was no longer Nelly-and-Reginald.

Nelly was sleeping hard, with a kind of determination, as if she had to use up a sleep that had lagged behind; not the sleep of the night before, for she was fresh, unfatigued, but a portion of sleep which she had not liquidated at the right time, which dated from her childhood, from some night of a ball, some journey when she had not been able to sleep on the train. This sleep had no relation to Reginald, he could tell: it was an old duty, an old debt. But that it should appear at a moment of such complete love, in their bright and sensitive passion, that it should loom so dim and indifferent between them now—Reginald could not understand it. He touched her, he caressed her, he ran his lips over the back of her neck, over her shoulders. Nelly slept on, her breathing quick and regular, but you could tell it would have to stop as soon as that portion of alien life was over and she fell back into her real life. By what word, what gesture had Reginald not so much changed as detached Nelly from himself, from everything?

It was as if there were a point, a lever he had only to press in order to have Nelly without his love. Nelly without his love was this scarcely living form plunged into a shadow of eternity, this body which did not respond to his caresses yet did not refuse them. She was receding from him, in a tide which washed her out of his arms. He felt alone, suddenly filled with apprehension; seeing Nelly as she had been before him, as she would be after him, completely stripped Reginald of that daily garment of love he had not taken off in four months. This love, this plaything suddenly escaped him too. He realized how anxious this love was, how full of pity, examining them both from somewhere in the room, as though to see, with a new kind of curiosity, what kind of couple it had entrusted itself to this time.

All at once he felt that Nelly was awake. The portion of sleep left over from the night when the little girl had been kept awake by quarrelling neighbors—people quarrel at night!—or from the night her father had died, had been completely used up, and with a conviction she would never have had at the time. There was no doubt about it. Her breathing had been disengaged from its purifying role. He saw thoughts replacing dreams by imperceptible movements, and the silence which cloaked her body was a deliberate silence. Five minutes passed, about whose nature there could be no mistake: Nelly was no longer asleep. But why didn't she move, why didn't she inhale her love with the first breath of consciousness, as Reginald had thought she would, why did she remain without love beside him?—that is what he could not understand. Always when Nelly wakened, even when she was right beside him, she clung to Reginald; even before she was awake she seized that happiness and that passion which had nevertheless followed her into the very heart of her sleep. Today, nothing. Why was Reginald reminded of that girl he had seen in the Orient, a girl whom bandits had left naked at the roadside and who in her bitterness against fate, right there in front of her rescuers, remained lying where the bandits had left her, filled with rancor and not even bothering to put on her clothes. For a long while it seemed as though this love which had ventured out of Nelly circled around her, searching for a place where it could re-enter, and finding her body and her soul sealed against it.

As a matter of fact, Nelly was awake. She knew the nature of that sleep of hers. She knew it had been a kind of daze, the bewilderment which follows a blow on the head. She had no doubt that Reginald's accidental remark was that blow. She awakened in pain to this terrible truth: some day Reginald would know everything. If she hesitated to turn over, it was because she wanted to wait a little longer before seeing this new Reginald who was there behind her, who was no longer the eternal Reginald life had bound her to forever, but from now on a provisional Reginald of months, of weeks, perhaps of days. To go to bed with someone who is your whole life, your life forever, and to wake up with a temporary companion is a melancholy experience, and it was the experience Nelly had just had. Behind her was her old happiness, accumulated there against her back as though against a dam. Reginald was still immersed in it. One movement and he would be dry. And henceforth it would be a fugitive, threatened happiness. Those daily two hours intercalated into her poor ordinary life like the outcroppings of a sure, permanent, eternal life, would become hours divided into minutes, glimmerings, uncertainties. She was already counting their seconds. It would take—whereas up till now the sun had always informed them—clocks, watches, perhaps an alarm to waken them in the dismantled evenings.

She did not move. Not because she was searching for a pretext, making a plan. Her plan was ready: to let things go. Gaston would be leaving in a month or two. Until then she could relax. She would not vary. She would not betray. If she failed, it was because, even by taking a lie as far as it can go, you cannot make it into a truth. It was because consciousness, determination, audacity in deception cannot enslave it: who can say as much of sincerity? Confess everything to Reginald—never! He wouldn't understand. It would mean confessing a coincidence, an overlap between the two Nellys which did not exist. The only seams between them were the ones Nelly undertook to reduce to a minimum. A whole series of lies occurred to her, which she would certainly manage to tell him before the end—that she had come to him virginal, ignorant, unawakened. That even at a pool she had never seen a naked male buttock. That she had never spent the night with her husband: he didn't exist, she could say anything about him. All the things which Nelly felt to be the supreme truth, and which could be expressed only by lies. She would see what provocation produced. She would see if Reginald was worthy of her, if he dared follow her into a world rectified and made over according to the dignity of their love. She doubted he would. The man whom the weak and inadequate dam of her body contained behind her was merely the strongest, the simplest, the most generous of men: a miserable man, incapable of living in this splendid virgin forest of the world, merely cutting through it, with the truth for machete, pathetic paths where the serpent never lingers. Let him find out what life is!

But my God, how painful it was to think that now she would have to turn over and smile at what looked like so much disaster! He would turn her over himself, very well, let him! He would undertake to organize the confrontation, perfect! There, he was doing it. She could still smile at him, she wasn't out of lies yet. She could still kiss him. She could—though for the last moment she and Reginald represented two different races of love—get up and dress with the same movements, the corresponding garments.

Yet how strange it was, and how funny too, to find this couple in the taxi, the man encased in an armor of eternal love, starched with eternity, and the woman decked out in a terrible but uncertain love, an aura: the taxi was heading into the sunset, and the red beams, which the driver's body intercepted from Reginald, streamed over Nelly. It was very beautiful. But in the shadowy streets, she felt again that her love was remote from her, as it had been just now in the bedroom. She held her hand outside the taxi to reach the sun. She had to stretch her fingers.

Of course Gaston was waiting for her. He had not yet spoken about her son, but Helene had warned Nelly. One day or another, there would be The Explanation. But until then, she took advantage of the situation as much as she could. Since Gaston greeted her with just that delicacy a man reserves for a woman who has just rocked a child to sleep, who has just given suck, so much the worse for him! She would say nothing, one way or the other. Moreover, instinctively, out of love for this future child, she would never commit a blunder which might betray it. Long ago she had bought medical books to make sure it would arrive at the right time; she had gone on diets so that it would be strong. The fact that in Gaston's presence she now found means of showing she was well informed about measles, milk, or first aid was not a departure from the truth. The fact that she now affected a great fear of flies, which carry germs, of mosquitoes, which disfigure a baby's face in an hour, was hardly serious. The fact that poor Gaston virtually regarded this son's existence as a new virginity, that he venerated the arms which rocked it, the breasts which suckled it, the loins which carried it, was after all the real sentiment a man should have for a woman, symbol—mother or not—of maternity. Moreover it was curious to see how little she had to do in order to justify Gaston's fiction. Those who have compared Love to a child did not suspect how close they came. From her rendezvous with Reginald, Nelly returned with a gaiety, or an anxiety, or a melancholy, or an exultation which a shrewder man than Gaston, even seeing them so close to their source, might have attributed to maternal love.

From that point of view, then everything would be fine if Gaston didn't take it into his head to bring toys or to buy a little car: the other day he had stopped her in front of a kind of white-and-silver mail coach.

If only, my God! he didn't send it to Reginald or try to bribe the nurse to let him see the boy, his stepson . . . Gaston would be away for six months. Nelly would certainly have enough difficulties during his absence, if only from her mother, so that her letters would betray the difficulties a son causes. On his return, they would see . . . If she was too sad, if Reginald had gone, there would still be the recourse of being as sad as she liked, of wearing mourning, of saying the son had died. Henceforth she would always be entitled, with Gaston, to be solitary and sad when she wanted to. She would find, in some Parisian cemetery, a child's grave. The father's name didn't matter. Besides, perhaps there would really be a son—Reginald's son. What joy, what measureless joy! A little too young—Gaston, when he saw it later on, much later on, would think he was a little young, and would try to work out the dates. But that was a problem for the remote future. One day Nelly had bought a photograph of a baby, precisely because she wanted a son who looked like that. She left it around in her apartment.

Reassured on Gaston's side, she did not remain idle on Reginald's. On that side, there was no question of maneuvering, of waiting. She had to gather up, quickly gather up all she could put into love, the only love she would have on this earth. How she embellished it now, that factitious alcove she and Reginald had invented—he by his lack of curiosity, she by her desire to conceal the past—in which to house so true a passion, and with each new and sincere impulse that flung her toward Reginald, she hung up in it, like an *ex voto,* some new myth. She discovered that ten years ago Reginald had spent a month at Annecy. So she told him that she had been at the same hotel on the lake, that she had been thirteen, that she had seen him, and loved him, and that she had sworn never to love any other man. Given this point of departure, it was easy for her to offer Reginald's amazement nothing more than a life consecrated to Reginald . . . How comfortable it was, and how logical! How good it felt to pad the past with this love to which the future was denied! In all her memories, Reginald took up residence as if he had really been there. He was the stowaway of her entire adolescence. Every year, on Saint Reginald's Day, she had found an excuse to be alone. She had had engraved on a little gold watch—what a pity she had lost it—a motto her Latin teacher had written for her: *Regina per Reginaldum* . . . On her wedding day, she had worn a dress chosen for him. It had been so sweet, thinking of Reginald, saying that fatal yes, not so fatal, since her husband, that night, had tenderly embraced her and left her alone—as if it were Saint Reginald's Day . . . Only it was too bad Nelly had set this age at thirteen and forbidden her childhood to Reginald. But she would get him into it somehow.

That would be her lie to herself. Lying beside him when she was silent, she would be lying to herself, deciding that Reginald was there the first time she opened her eyes—she was about eight days old but she saw him . . . And he was there when she uttered her first cry; she had imitated a cat, her mother said. Reginald had guided her in that first language, sitting near the bassinet, mewing softly. And he had been there for the encounter with the supposedly mad dog—it was Reginald who had told the nurse not to run away, to climb that ladder. And now the whole life she had hitherto regarded with dry eyes, a dry soul, the life she considered the life of a hard, willful, deliberate little girl, gradually furnished her proofs that she might have been tender, soft, voluptuous. As a problem is solved by using some letter or figure which has nothing to do with the problem, by using Reginald now, the whole problem was solved. By adding Reginald to that childhood in which he had never existed, even to the memories least susceptible of tenderness, the memories she owed to her mother, to her brothers, she obtained this unique solution to the problem: love. And even when she subtracted Reginald, it turned out that love remained.

Reginald listened to her tenderly. He believed it all. Each time he was amazed to see that life had finally brought him this love he had renounced after so many experiments. When you reach the critical age, a woman of twenty-five who not only loves you alone but has never loved anyone else; who is unknown, and who has loved you since her childhood . . . It was the sequel to the little Portuguese girl! He did not see that Nelly invented this love which fit her so well, made it to measure every day, made it to order. Some days she didn't need to, so splendid was the energy of their passion, and there were some days when the truth was so perfect that lying couldn't have improved on it. But Nelly now demanded a first-class truth, a truth worthy of them, and that wasn't easy. Sometimes, in the street, in a restaurant, she was suddenly overcome by pride, the pride of women who feel that their love, that day, is the first in Paris. On certain days, she felt that it was the first in the world. She insisted on that first rank—she became irritable as soon as it was threatened. It was then that by a word, by an invention, she restored it to its class of perfection, guessing admirably by Reginald's mood if on that day she should have run away from boarding school at eleven or tried to commit suicide at fifteen. Moreover she asked nothing better than to say nothing, to listen to Reginald, who also became talkative, who answered each of these rather imaginary tales with a true one, who had a childhood, a mother, friends on whom lying had no more effect than bindweed on a walnut tree. It is no problem, moreover, lying to someone you love, to the man you love. He is the only one you can lie to joyfully, gratefully.

With Gaston, each lie seemed to her as gross, as burdensome as . . . as her feelings for Gaston. It wouldn't have been worth the trouble, if it weren't the condition, the ransom of Reginald's love. With

Reginald, what was each lie compared to their love: a wave in the sea, a grain of sand! She resented Gaston for the lies he made her tell: they spoiled her life with Reginald. She was grateful to Reginald for inspiring her to embellish her past. What relation could there be between that false language which concealed it from Gaston, which saved it from the worst, and the kind which adorned it, which prepared it for Reginald?

What was inexplicable was that melancholy, that anxiety which increased precisely in proportion as it should have diminished, for Gaston was now leaving in two weeks. Where was the threat coming from? She didn't know, but there was a threat somewhere. There were afternoons when she felt that her love was not the first, now, but the most threatened in Paris. There were days when she was so exhausted from shifting from one man to the other, from keeping them apart, that she almost wished Gaston and Reginald would not persist in living on different continents but would meet, mingle, make friends. Married women with lovers don't know how lucky they are, especially when that lover and that husband know each other. The threat must be coming from herself, from a fatigue which couldn't wait for Gaston's departure. Nelly was no longer sure of herself, she felt herself growing impatient—an impatience that caused certain confusions: for the first time she had been cross with Reginald and momentarily tender with Gaston. She had realized this too late, and quickly made up for it, but both men had been stupefied, and she felt that ever since this blunder both were living on that moment, which had been, for each of them, a revelation.

Yet one day there was a diversion: Reginald told her about one of his friends who was a liar.

"How can you tell a liar?" Nelly asked.

"You can tell this one by his eyes. They bulge."

"Did he lie to you?"

"To everyone. I would run into him in the street. He looked pleased. I asked him why. It was because he had just given a Cézanne watercolor to a friend who adored it. The friend was moved to tears. He had never expected to be given a Cézanne watercolor . . ."

"And your friend hadn't given it to him?"

"He had never had one. All he had in his room were two chairs and an old mattress and a sick sister. But he kept giving away Cézannes, Rodins, Renoirs . . . Once he slipped a magnificent Inca charm into the bag of a pretty woman who passed him on the street!"

"Had he inherited the Inca charm from his family?"

"An old gentleman who had a ranch in Guatemala had found the charm in a place called Gaxerco. He had lost it, my friend found it. A year later they met at the Lost & Found."

"Why?"

"My friend was coming to claim the charm after a year. The old gentleman was coming back from his year in Guatemala, but he was so happy that he gave it to my friend. And it brought my friend luck—the day he gave it away he met his fiancée."

"Is that true?"

"Not one word. His fiancée—he showed me her picture last week—is an Englishwoman who lives in London—she has a drop of Spanish blood, and you can't imagine how well her English complexion goes with those Spanish eyes. My friend adores her, and she adores him. So does her daughter—she has a daughter. He's in heaven, all because he's going to be living with a child of six!"

"And what does he do now?"

"He runs a little bookshop on the corner of the Rue des Saints-Pères."

Nelly went that very evening to the Rue des Saints-Pères. She visited two or three shops, quickly discovered that the booksellers there lied only to conceal their income from the tax collector or the pages missing from a first edition. They were obscene, with their barefaced lies! But in the fourth shop, there could be no mistake about it. The liar was there. A very nice liar. Very well-dressed, though with piping and spats. What could be the use of those magnificent spats? The business of selling first editions or the exercise of lying? He wasn't like Nelly, he had props: an enormous ring with an Egyptian inscription, tortoise-shell glasses sticking out of his pocket, a huge silk handkerchief like the ones the gaucho in the circus or perhaps on the pampas, just for his personal pleasure, flicks out of his girl's hand with his whip. A charming gold-headed cane was lying across the desk, lying . . . She would find out if he could lie. She invented a name. "The Marquise de Saanedra told me you'd be sure to have the book I'm looking for."

"Such a charming woman!"

*

* *

To warn Reginald. Yes, she had to warn Reginald. But how? By telling him everything, or almost everything: that would be the end, or in any case a mortal risk. By writing him an anonymous letter, by gradually forcing him to see; then he would decide what he wanted, he would choose. But why not wait these two weeks until Gaston left? For two months of this perfect happiness, what wouldn't she do? Yet there was one thing—it was so simple: the one thing was The Miracle. She was surprised to discover she had not yet renounced what she had counted on all her life: The Miracle.

Moreover there were twenty possible ones. The miracle-worker had his choice. One day Reginald could just say: "Darling, if you're married, get a divorce. If you're a widow, get ready. We're getting married. If you've had other affairs, I know they didn't count. It's not your fault if I came so late. If you've tried to keep them from me, it's still my fault. Order your dress. I'll apply for the license . . ." Or else Gaston would stop being kind, tender; Gaston would get furious, would brutalize her . . . Or else she would forget everything, one morning she would wake up having forgotten everything, and Gaston would have forgotten everything, and she would meet Reginald by accident, she would take care of the rest whether it was in the street, at the theatre, in Venezuela or in Saint-Germain.

But the first one was the real Miracle: Reginald could work it all by himself, without any divine discourse.

However there was another one, the Gaston Miracle.

9

When Gaston—who the day before his departure had insisted on delivering the little car in person at the address given him by the detective agency he had hired to follow Nelly, and indeed had delivered it, as though by an *accouchement,* from his own car as if it were the daughter of that enormous vehicle—when Gaston saw his chauffeur bringing it back with a downcast expression, he immediately anticipated the worst. Not that the child was dead; Nelly had been particularly gay the day before. Not that the child did not like cars. But—as the chauffeur himself immediately told him, moreover—there was no child in the house. Or rather, there were two, who happened to be playing outside the concierge's window—Gaston could see them there now, a redhead with a harelip, and another very dirty boy who said his name was Cécel—Marcel, obviously.

Gaston cautiously approached; saw the tree in the

courtyard, saw the black sock on the tree, did not suspect he was overlooking one of Nelly's affections, brushed by the two children to enter the concierge's apartment—how light children are!—learned that the lady who came every day was named Madame Reginald, the gentleman Monsieur Reginald, that as a matter of fact, despite a praiseworthy daily persistence, they had as yet no children—there's still time, Gaston said, to make the concierge laugh, and as a matter of fact she laughed—and that if he would come back around five he would be sure to find them at home. It would be the first visit they had received in the six months they had been coming every day. Gaston still had his doubts. "I must be mistaken," he said. "Is Madame Reginald blonde or dark?"

"There she is," the concierge said. "My son's a photographer, he comes Sundays and he took that without her knowing it."

Gaston saw Nelly, in her motherly dress, but with an expression he did not recognize. Everything he had ever dreamed of seeing in Nelly—unconsciously, since he thought she was perfect—was there. Gentleness, submission, bliss had accumulated on her face in a cream so thick that the concierge's son had been able to skim off a layer without anything being missed. The wind was blowing. Nelly stood on the curb as though on a prow. Yes, that was it. Gaston, who in his total ignorance remembered only the parts which happened to be missing from Greek statues, could not help thinking Nelly had the head and arms and the foot of the

Victory of Samothrace. There was no doubt about it, the hard, flirtatious, indifferent woman he worshipped was tender, simple, passionate. But not for Gaston. Even that half-raised leg meant: I'm rising. Rising from boredom toward my one occupation. Rising out of the mud toward love. Rising from Gaston, my left leg is still on Gaston, but about to leave him. Once upstairs, once on high, I shall remove my shoe, since it has walked on Gaston. Look, Reginald, how my smile rinses this face Gaston has kissed, how this black dress on my body, with this little scarf round my neck, erases all the marks Gaston has left on me . . . Gaston recognized the little scarf, it was purple. That was a mistake. In the photograph, you could not tell. But the purple had no effect, erased nothing from Nelly's neck. If she had worn purple garters, a purple slip, nothing at all would have been eliminated. But it was her face which was the enigma for Gaston, that kind, generous, open face. The face of the Medusa, he would have said.

He took the photograph, paid more for it than for a dozen of the huge profiles in which Nelly offered the world, though in her best dress, the indifference she reserved for everything concerning Gaston—the other profile would be smiling, promising—and left. He had to pass through the children. He even had to separate them, for they were fighting now. He accidentally touched the little redhead's harelip. It was hard, coarse, a place in the world ready-made for misery . . . The car was waiting, its little car back in its womb . . . Gaston did not have the strength to get in, it would have seemed like getting into the little car. He sent it away, and walked through the neighborhood.

Nelly's neighborhood. He looked at it, from the curb where Nelly stepped back down into boredom, disgust, obligation, stepped back down to Gaston. He saw the little realm that was Nelly's. The bakery where Nelly bought her strawberry tarts, he recognized the crust, one day when Nelly must have been in a hurry she had bought them here, so good he had asked for the address. Now he had it. Nelly's grocery, where she had been less fortunate: the cheese was too hard. Nelly's sewing shop, in the window were buttons, pins, thread, yarn: everything with which Nelly could repair the ravages of her toilette. Nelly's stationery shop: here she bought her evening papers and, each week, *Les Echos de la Semaine*. Nelly's florist. Yes, he noticed now: among whatever was tasted, smelled, read at Nelly's, there were dishes, flowers, newspapers which were not better or more beautiful than the rest, but for which she had less severity, a kind of indulgence. They were the ones she had bought here in her realm, the eggs, the magazines, the little scarf, the stockings of her realm. A corkscrew appeared one day which Nelly cherished as if it were a brooch, a buttonhook she would not let Gaston touch. All the household repairs, Gaston had noticed, as well as her having her wristwatch cleaned, her shoes resoled—such things were no longer done by her local tradesmen but here, in her real neighborhood.

He walked back, saw the tree again. The sock

swayed in the breeze. From her window Nelly would have had to see that sock. Sparrows were hopping from branch to branch, sparrows Nelly had seen, whose cheeping had awakened Nelly. And this whole neighborhood was ready, though Nelly arrived only at five: the newsstand was displaying its noon editions, which Nelly had never sampled, the grocer was setting out his noon milk, which Nelly would never drink, and his pippins, which Nelly did not care for, his tangerines, which she detested . . . All so that one afternoon, out of the enormous selection maintained at great expense by Les Halles, Nelly could detach a Golden Delicious, a Camembert, or a copy of *Vogue*. Perhaps among all these fruits was the peach Nelly would eat tonight . . . Tonight? Which night? Enough of that! There were the things Gaston had to buy for his trip. He had to leave!

Gaston tried to escape from the circle, but failed. To buy a plaid wool lap robe at the moment you discover that the woman you love has made you believe she has a son so she can meet her lover undisturbed, is a difficult operation. To select a white seersucker jacket without pocket flaps on the morning you have bought a toy car for your wife's lover, is simply not done. Gaston would never have guessed that alarm clocks, socks, aspirin, shoe trees could lead so directly to the heart, the mind, the eyes, almost to tears. Especially when the street sloped up. His legs were weak, like the day he had to kneel in the Madeleine as best man . . . Weddings! Why did he think of a wedding, of a bride, of husband and wife . . . Why were people bumping into him? If Gaston had been with someone who felt the way he did now, a good man flouted, reviled, sacrificed, he would have given him a helping hand, especially on a hill, would have taken his arm . . . No, people bumped into him, even grazed him with a plank; a retired admiral stuck his cane under his arm, to put out Gaston's eye.

To wound, to blind Gaston—what was the good of that? Yet that was all humanity could offer him right now. If the trees lining the sidewalk had suddenly burst into wonderful blossoms for him, or magnificent socks, or orchids, if all the concierge's phonographs, instead of whining out nonsense, had suddenly intoned a hymn in his honor, if the sky had filled with stars, with flashes of lightning to greet him, if that statue of Jules Favre had come alive, had stepped toward him, had embraced him, if all the employees of the Renault works, bearing huge banners with Gaston's name in Gothic letters, had turned into cherubs and floated through the air chanting that name, it would have been the least humanity could do for him. He would not have been comforted by it, but he would have been touched. If the windows on every floor had opened and all the young women and girls there and in the street had acclaimed him, had pelted him with flowers, had understood him, if that woman passing—she wasn't bad-looking—had taken his arm, dragged him home with her, to a palace, to a hovel, had soothed him, washed him, dried him—washed him with misery, dried him with opprobrium—she really wasn't bad-looking at all—that would have been a minimum. But nothing, no help, no rescue, no relief for this exhausted man . . . Yes. That horse.

Gaston liked horses. He had been a corporal in the Quartermaster Corps of the Provins Cuirassiers. This one wasn't a cavalry horse. It would have collapsed under Gaston, who had put on some weight since his military service. But since the question was not to mount the horse but to be rescued by it—the problem did not arise. Gaston had often seen men leading horses by the bridle through the traffic to an ignominious death on the outskirts of Paris. But none had attracted his attention so sharply. The other horses seemed to have given up, to have submitted to an increasingly ignoble life, to have abandoned the struggle. Gaston, who knew the habits of horses, was not mistaken: this one did not understand, its every movement seemed to say that it was changing its way of life, that it understood it was changing its way of life. The horse had some breeding, you could see that, and its terrible emaciation even emphasized a certain elegance in its legs, its hindquarters, though an old scar on the right rear pastern betrayed a certain weakness the animal concealed by a kind of swaying leg movement which would have been affected at an earlier time of its life. It could never have been a cavalry horse—it passed close by a noisy phonograph without pricking up its ears; like the horses and men who have not done their military service, it was not too mistrustful. Some little old English carriage horse, given away to an itinerant suburban painter, then to some peddler, another peddler, each more ignoble than the last—milk, rags, scrap iron . . . This was the last transition . . .

The man was short, stocky, wearing a blue smock and a cap, but he was very clean and his gestures were very confident. He kept his hand as near the nostrils as possible. The horse felt absolutely secure. Gaston noticed that the horse was trying to anticipate the man's slightest intentions. At the least pressure, it turned left, right, stopped. Nor did it permit itself, as it must have done once, the slightest personal judgment. How good it was to be led! How good this man was, who so authoritatively divided the mass of pedestrians! What a pleasure it was to follow him! The finest couple in the world is always a man and a horse, even when the horse is slightly, ever so slightly, lopsided. In order to flatter the man and make him think he was walking fast, though its gait was precisely that of a short man walking, the horse began to trot. It trotted standing, but the man, not even winded, would think from its gait that he was walking faster than a trotting horse. Each time they stopped, Gaston saw the horse glance at the man, as though regretfully. Obviously this was a master who did not talk much, who did not caress the animal much, but after all, that was the horse's fault. It had been foolish those ten years when its mistress had tried to kiss it on the nostrils and it tossed its head to escape her. And foolish with the painter, who kept putting tassels on it. If this man wanted to put tassels on it, or even to caress its ears, which were sensitive, let him, let him . . . Yes, starting today, things would be different . . . It would try to get along with men, it had not understood them, it would no longer rear against the sides of the stall: what was the use of rearing against the sides of a stall . . . Now the man made it stop short to avoid a skidding car. By a single gesture, he had saved the horse from an accident. There was no denying it: men were good.

Gaston had reached the top of the street, he had crossed the frontier of Nelly's realm. The horse had hauled Gaston into a world where the shops, the newsstands had never seen Nelly. Its role was over. What good would it have done Gaston to follow, to accompany it to the end of that avenue into which turned, heading toward the same fate, a long row of horses? What would this horse think, seeing that row? That it was a day of reconciliation between men and horses? Or that its master was going to leave it with the others, abandon it in herd just when it imagined it had left the herd forever? Gaston would have suffered at that—already he felt how disappointed the little horse was . . . But it must be something else. The man did not let the horse go. He simply walked faster. The little horse trotted, really trotted now, already it was tired, but the trot told what kind of horse it was . . . And it vanished, its faded chestnut devoured by the black, the white and the bay of the poor equine buttocks in which Gaston saw all of human life.

What was he going to do, hoisted up by such a

savior on to the platform where there was nothing left of Nelly? Go see Nelly? He thought of going to see Nelly for a moment, of making her lie to him. In the Sahara—Gaston had been a sergeant-major in the Spahis—they used to catch horned vipers and make them spit out their venom. They would spit out enough to soak a whole rag. After that, the viper could bite, but it was only a bite. If Gaston had made Nelly lie now, her lies would be harmless. He would have no difficulty leaving her forever, with the rag. Suppose he tried right now, by telephone. He went into a post office—it was four in the afternoon. Nelly would be home changing from her lunch dress to her son's dress. He would catch her changing skins.

"Hello," Nelly said.

How knowing you become, once you know. That "hello" meant nothing. But it was full of deception. "It's me—Gaston. What are you doing?"

If Nelly had not lied, this would have been her answer, in either of the two cases Gaston considered: "What am I doing? Right now, I'm getting dressed to see Reginald, to lie down beside him, to undress. I'm putting on the clothes I take off to be with Reginald. What am I doing? In my life, I'm leading a double, no, not a double but an alternating life. Each one has its truth, but the two together are a lie . . . I'm lying, that's what I'm doing."

But Nelly could not answer the truth, since she was lying. "Nothing. You?"

What was he doing? He was following a horse

being led to the slaughterhouse. He was giving toy cars to his fiancée's lover. He was doing what fools do.

"Are you going out? Do you want to come out with me?"

"What shall we do?"

Quickly, incomprehensibly, Gaston said: "Something very different from what you do with Reginald."

"What?"

Nelly, of course, had not understood. But the sound of the sentence must have had something alarming in it. It echoed too closely the sentence she was saying to herself. Gaston went on: "Something interesting like going to the cinema."

Poor Gaston. He wasn't very resourceful about assonance. His family claimed descent from Thibaut de Champagne. On the female side, of course. Women are always there, when transmission and mediation are involved. But Thibaut de Champagne would certainly have found a closer assonance than *Reginald* and *cinema*. Besides, Nelly wasn't stupid; she understood immediately that there was danger in the air, or a possibility of danger.

"Fine. I'm getting dressed. Will you call for me?"

She was getting dressed. That meant she was putting back on the dress already discarded, she was getting out of the brown or black skirt.

"You don't have to go see your little protégé?"

"I've already been."

How well she lied! "All the teeth have come in, the measles are over, the diaper rash gone?"

"What's the matter with you, Gaston?"

"Nothing. I'll be there in a few minutes." And perhaps he would have been there in a few minutes, if he had not found, waiting for him outside the post office, what can protect you from disaster even more efficaciously than a horse on its way to the slaughterhouse. For you cannot get onto a horse on its way to the slaughterhouse, nor get inside it. Whereas you got on, you got inside this new rescue, this new savior: a bus. Not many passengers inside: at four in the afternoon, the emigration to Montsouris was not at its height. What it came down to was a professor on his way to inaugurate the cafeteria at the Cité Universitaire, a dealer in Leeds porcelain who had spent the day in pursuit of a basin just arrived from England, a young Montsourissoise who had just delivered the MMC underwear models to her workshop, a crippled veteran who gave the journey its period flavor, and a fat woman embellished with a peony. Precisely the contrary of the ark, precisely the persons who would have perished first in the Flood, and who were thus saved from the movement of the boulevards.

The bus followed a carefully planned itinerary which allowed it to avoid both wealthy neighborhoods and slums. This continuous bath in a mediocrity of architecture, class, and profession soothed Gaston. At the stops, only those human beings were taken on or transferred of whom humanity could be neither proud nor ashamed, who were neither handsome nor ugly, neither wicked nor saintly. All were calm, none raised the question of lying, none suddenly clutched at your heart until you almost cried out. A single incident. A man in a jacket got on, realized he had made a mistake, wanted the bus to stop because he caught sight of the bus he wanted to take going diagonally, yanked at the cord, shoved the conductor out of the way. People going through Paris diagonally instead of straight ahead are less insupportable than liars, but just barely. It was a relief once he had gone. Besides, he missed his own bus, as is inevitably the case with things which belong to you and for which you have made sacrifices, risked your life, insulted your fellow men.

Past the park, there were only two people on the bus, Gaston and a young woman who was nibbling on a fig newton. Whereby she interested Gaston, a specialist in aliments and textiles, for a fig newton belonged to the realm of which he was the ruler, whereas if she had eaten dozens of chocolate eclairs or cream puffs, she remained marginal to verifiable aliments, to human nourishment. Gaston, by various stratagems, glimpsed the manufacturer's name. It was the name of a firm he controlled. He felt more comfortable with this person whose flour he had sifted and who was eating a fig newton bearing his initials. In Gaston's circumstances, a man is sensitive to the slightest attentions. This was one of them. Especially since the young woman, having finished the first fig newton, took a second one out of the package, and Gaston was proud of that, for he had protested at the last board meeting against the proposed suppression of this particular fig newton, certain adversaries claiming that the future was in gingersnaps . . . Gaston followed the young woman's deglutition with the anxiety of those who suspect poison in their food. He was quickly reassured, moreover, for she took a third fig newton. This was perhaps the first time Gaston had ever seen one of his products consumed under his very eyes. As a matter of fact, he had almost never seen one of the two billion human beings whose nourishment or whose garments he supervised. In Gaston's circles, he saw precisely those demigods or demigoddesses who are exempt from statistical laws, who have private cooks, private tailors, not overseers of humanity, and who are related to major economic currents only by the gasoline in their cars. An alimentary god, Gaston saw one of his creatures at the moment of deglutition, the most important moment next to that of procreation. He was touched: Nelly disdained his bakeries and his department stores. Especially since this young woman—there could be no mistake about it—was also dressed by Gaston. It was one of his Roanne prints, a dress cut from the material meant for Iraq and Burma, a small consignment of which Gaston had deflected to his French market. The shoes too seemed to be from Limoges. By the eyelets you could have sworn they were Limoges, but those Fougère people steal your ideas for eyelets quite shamelessly. Gaston was really moved. For the first time he discovered what he had never been able to find in his own world, that world of ten thousand persons who kept from him the hundreds of millions to whom he distributed rice or quinine. Finding a representative in this modest form here on the Montsouris bus was anything but disagreeable. To Nelly he had never been able to offer an object made by his factories, for her he was as remote from his metals, his glutens, his silks as an ant or a Nibelung. That red dress in which she was waiting for him now, anxious and outraged, did not owe one thread or one dyestuff to Gaston, who had clothed this young person opposite him, fed her, shod her. It was as if—almost—he had given all his presents to her. He smiled at her.

Meanwhile Norma Coldeau, sitting opposite Gaston and devouring her fig newtons, was wondering how she could get hold of more cocaine. The supply was particularly short, since at present she was returning from a visit to the Prefecture of Police, where her clothes and her person had been conscientiously searched. Perhaps this man had some? She naturally remembered having seen him somewhere, for Norma, in the presence of any man or woman, always had some reminiscence, true or false, of hours spent together in the utmost intimacy. In the oddest countenance she recognized features indelibly marked on her memory. Only children's faces seemed to her terribly unfamiliar, and she avoided them like the plague. Innocence and shyness seemed to her filled with incalculable threats. When she passed one of those smiling little girls in the park, or one of those polite boys hustling the sidewalk in the name of some unimaginable freedom of purity, Norma was disgusted. She would scarcely have recognized her own mother or her nephew under those fearful signs. But any man, any woman offered her a face she had known in the worst torpor of the worst paroxysm, a face she could not distinguish from the face of all other men, all other women. So that facing Gaston, Norma offered no defense, no flirtation, nor did she feel any attraction. Facing Gaston, she was in the state of a woman facing the man who has possessed her as many times as she has had lovers, *i.e.,* in the present case, exactly as many as there are grains of sand on the seashore. She answered him with a smile which Gaston took for an invitation and which was the vague smile of politeness to the nightly lover. Then she turned away, suddenly distracted, with a distraction which Gaston read as a disdain for men and which was merely a proof of familiarity with them. Then she got off the bus with a familiar gesture for this man who had taken her virginity, who had slept three thousand times against her body, who had satiated and tormented her, who had made her sew on buttons at three in the morning, buy sliced ham at seven, ring the bells of all-night pharmacies to buy milk of bismuth, who had pinned her under the wreckage of a car—five months in the hospital, a perforated eardrum—who had smeared her with tar and stuck stork feathers into it for Mardi Gras at Saint-Tropez, who had kept her four days in Marrakech like a pasha in his harem from which she had escaped by sleeping with a eunuch, who had made her parachute out of a plane and fire a round of machine-gun bullets two hundred yards up in the air, who had on the other hand as a student at Alfort taken her cat to Alfort when it had cat fever, who as a surgeon had operated on that same cat, even though he charged ten thousand francs for an appendicitis operation—Norma leaned on Gaston's shoulder and pinched his biceps . . .

"Where are you going?" Gaston asked.

Where? Then she didn't know him so well as she thought. Doubtless he belonged to that male part of the world to which she gave herself only in hotels. This narrowed the horizon. She was no longer dealing with the man who forced her to swallow all the jewels he gave her, the one who wept on her shoulder so hard that all the henna in her hair had run, the one who for a whole month had refused to give her a white fox and goldfish, which she obtained a few days later, by the way, when she thought of asking for them separately, the one who had been decent enough to tell the manager that he had broken the big mirror when it was her fault, the one who had braided her hair—it was always your hair they were after—into nautical knots, in the days when she wore her hair long, the one who had even died in her arms, bright red all over. Moreover he was the only dead man she had ever seen, the only member of that race with scarlet faces and blood red hands which the dead were for Norma. Perhaps she had better explain. "Home. You coming?"

"Home?"

Now she knew. She recognized that voice. It was the voice of the one who grabbed her by the feet and swung her round as fast as he could; or maybe it was the one who had locked her in a wardrobe from which she had been rescued by the merest chance; or maybe —it had to be the one—who had first made her wear a kimono and red leather slippers with pointed toes, who had sprayed the room with Journée d'Ivresse, and had given her her first opium pipe. She took Gaston's arm, who little suspected that, for this woman stuffed with Fig Newtons Gaston, he represented a man who provides opium and cocaine.

How brave, how proud he was! When the others brought the stuff, powdered or mixed, they were afraid to be seen with her—she had already been picked up, and usually they had been arrested a few times too. But this one was a real man. He didn't avoid the cop on the corner who had been to her place with so many search warrants. He breathed quite calmly, he stopped to look at the ducks in the pond. Sometimes he trembled all over, sometimes a sigh rose to his lips which Norma recognized as a kind of sob—her mother had that same habit of sighing instead of sobbing, they thought she was having an asthma attack when she was really crying—but that was probably because he hadn't smoked yet this morning. Besides he wasn't bad-looking. He looked like the one who had made the cop take a sniff, only more sure of himself, more serious. She admired the way he walked in broad daylight like an owl who suddenly starts enjoying the sun. He had, all at once, what she had never found combined in any one person: hidden treasure and open strength. She trusted him, she trusted him so much that for a moment she took advantage of her confidence as though it was a drug stronger than all the others, enjoyed that light on the conservatory, those plumes of smoke from the train which seemed to be coming out of the trees, all of which she took for an effect of the drug, the only puff of pure air she had inhaled for years. And the emotion was so strong that for the first time in a long time she felt like making love. Walking beside Norma, Gaston entrusted himself to her just as he had entrusted himself, a little while ago, to the horse . . . Where was that horse now? He entrusted himself, or thought he entrusted himself, to simplicity, to hard times, to the normal life of ordinary people. That was how they took each other's arm, each thinking the other contained the contrary of what was actually there; Norma suddenly attached to this man by everything her life had had to do with men, by a distant past; Gaston to a new being who resembled none of the women he had ever known or who had ever known him, who belonged to the race of neither his cousins nor his mistresses nor his wife, nor Nelly.

Kill himself? He would see later on. There would always be time to kill himself for Nelly. Yes, for a man who absolutely insisted on killing himself, there was something he could do: he could die before that horse. For the first time in all the thousands of years during which animals have been sacrificed to men, he could sacrifice himself for an animal. That so much blood should have flowed over the earth—Gaston, who also had interests in a cannery, knew how much blood an ox contains, and a cow, and a lamb, and a wretched, anemic horse—and that men had never paid homage to those millions of beasts which had perished consciously or unconsciously in order to feed or amuse humanity, was an injustice so great that it would have been worth his while for a man really determined to die to make reparation, to arrange to die ahead of a doomed animal. When would they slaughter the little horse? Tomorrow morning at dawn. They only slaughter horses at night during a famine. So in order to be sure he preceded it, to be sure that for once a man would precede the cortege of beasts to their subterranean realm, Gaston would have to kill himself around the time day begins, when cocks crow, he would have to set his alarm for four, for instance. Fifteen minutes to wake up one last time, fifteen minutes to shave, to wash, and then he could . . . But to die for Nelly, no. To die for what is not pure, what is not true, what you cannot caress without reservations, what you cannot touch without fear, no. Fifteen minutes could remain for the little horse, fifteen minutes waiting behind the others, advancing step by step, no longer feeling hungry because it hadn't eaten for two days, wondering what meadow that door would lead to, opening up ahead, letting through only ten horses at once. Now it had missed its turn. It had been the eleventh.

Now it was the first. It was like all the other horses, but a man had decided not to live longer than this one horse, had rendered it immortal . . . Now the door was open. Now . . .

Now that was what Gaston was thinking as he climbed Norma's staircase. Of preceding the cortege of mongooses struck down protecting us from cobras, of bulls massacred, of horses slaughtered, quickly overtaken by their dim ghosts, by the galloping ghost of the little horse. The stairs were steep. Norma was hanging on his arm. At each landing she kissed him. Through the doors on the landings he heard voices, the voices of families washing, scolding children, chopping meat. They had only to open their doors to see this man who two hours ago was engaged to a woman who loved him, being kissed now by a kind of fiancée who had suddenly risen up at the frontier of Norma's realm and of other realms. It was really the idea of the groom coming home with his bride which overwhelmed Gaston. It had never occurred to him that when he brought Nelly home there would be an elevator. He had thought only of the stairs, with landings they would hurry past, a staircase where all those forbidden kisses he had given Nelly would become sanctified kisses, a staircase at the foot of which Nelly would still be his somewhat compromised, slightly suspect fiancée, and at the summit of which, by the time he put her down on the bed, she would turn into a woman sparkling with purity, with virginity. Nelly! What dreadful sloth, not to be busy with Nelly! Usually when he was separated from her, it seemed to Gaston that he could see her better than ever. Sometimes, knowing where she was going, he would station himself in order to watch her pass, the way an automobile manufacturer stands on a corner to see his own car pass. How stupid these comparisons with cars were! But in any case, he saw Nelly better from a distance, from farther away. How well he saw her now, from Norma's room!

Norma's room happened to be in order. A member of the narcotics squad, during the routine morning visit, had emptied and cleaned the tub, had given the room, while he was waiting for the inspector who didn't like a mess, the kind of order which his own wife, a policeman's wife, kept at home. Gaston was charmed by this orderliness due to the police: he attributed it to the innate genius of the working class. The policeman had hung up the clothes usually strewn over the chairs. The policeman had put back the brass bed which Norma had leaned against the wall to do her Swedish calisthenics. The policeman had managed, out of the black-glass and mother-of-pearl stands, to reconstruct what was for him the one indispensable piece of furniture at night, a night-table. The policeman had found two cane chairs, the ones Norma had borrowed from the Lithuanian student across the hall to put her spirit-lamp on; the policeman had arranged them on either side of the bridge table, no longer used to block the broken kitchen window. The policeman had sewn up the two holes Norma had poked in the green felt to get some air. Finally, not knowing what to do with the empty tin cans which lay around the floor, the policeman had stacked them, in order of size, in the Louis XV bookcase. So that Norma's moral nourishment seemed precisely that physical nourishment Gaston attributed to her. The classics of this charming little working girl, he thought, were his own olive oil, his own fish, his own pickles. He looked at this flesh fed on the fruits of the earth.

Norma had taken Gaston's hat and gloves with some ceremony, for accustomed as she was to the lovemaking of intoxicated men for whom the worst exhaustion is undressing, he was already naked for her. The jacket, the uniform, sometimes the frogged blue overcoats worn by her most up-to-date friends, constituted, in Norma's eyes, male nudity. On the other hand, she had to adapt herself, once these gloves and this hat were off, and to show her own nakedness. It could not be more complete. As they were, then and there, the two of them looked like the couple who have arranged an adulterous rendezvous for divorce proceedings, and who are waiting, in the most complete mutual indifference, for the three knocks from the police inspector. Gaston relished this dishonor.

10

Not for one moment could Reginald have suspected Nelly's anxiety. She appeared precisely on time for the same hours of oblivion and eternity, and tomorrow's joy was apparent in the somewhat melancholy smile of today's separation. Yet Gaston gone was much more disturbing than Gaston in the flesh. The throng of lies which flocked from all sides to help her was of no use, since Gaston was not here. From the concierge, Nelly learned the story of the little car, and that was all. She knew Gaston knew. At first she thought he had already left for America. That would have been too simple. Then that he had killed himself. Then that he was wandering around Paris somewhere, and she wondered if he would suddenly loom up in front of his rival, or perhaps he was shadowing Nelly, step by step . . . She did not turn around, so that she would not have to change her route. It was at one of these moments that she realized, with a joy which almost brought tears to her eyes, that if her words were sometimes false, her gestures never were. She had the impression that Gaston was behind her, and she was going to Reginald, and nothing in her movements suggested that she was not going to Reginald. She did not miss a turn, she took the sidewalks, the parks, the straightest route which ever led to Reginald. She did not change her expression. She greeted the newspaper vendor, the grocer who sold what he called "living sugar," which gave Nelly the same remorse when she put it in the tea as when she dropped a lobster into boiling water. And with Gaston too, really, she had never lied in her actions. Mute, she would have been incomparably candid. As she was to any viewer remote enough to miss her words. Was that the solution: never to speak? She had never spoken to herself, that was why she always thought of herself as candid. She spoke to herself less and less. She enjoyed following the truth of her life, which had led her so directly to Reginald. The summer was at its zenith. She went straight to all the desires of her body, a glass of cold water, a shower, a silk dress, as though to so many truths. But then, when a voice was raised in that silence to speak another truth—Reginald I love you, Reginald you are my life!—of course that combination of truths became something voluptuously insupportable, and the world of speech recovered an incomparable power over the world of silence.

It was at the core of these hours which Reginald still regarded as a human paradise, hours in which were already assembled drama, death perhaps, in any case disaster for one or the other two, that Nelly savored, the more clearly she saw its uncertainty, the fulfillment of her happiness. That silly Reginald accepted her caresses, her gazes, her silences as if they were the caresses, the gazes, the silences of the past, whereas now they were given to him by love itself. He never knew how lucky he was. If he had inquired into the real nature of those two hours he persisted in regarding as a retreat, a revenge, a repose, he would have seen that they burst into flame, that they scorched the day, the year, that all the other hours were consecrated to them, that they were love itself. It was his own gestures which lied, or were not true. He continued to make the little gestures of meeting, of understanding, whereas he spoke only of loving, of love; while Nelly, in her silence, made love each day in the exaltation of a victim and of a votary. Reginald thought he was taking her in his arms when she arrived, which was not true: Nelly rushed against him, so powerful was the impulse which had flung her there. She had bumps to show for it! Reginald thought he was kissing her; Nelly found, with her lips, what are sweetest and most terrible of all, other lips! Reginald thought he loved her; Nelly found the end of everything, the reason for everything, death.

All this was so powerful that sometimes Reginald's person was almost eliminated by it. Not that she could have imagined anyone else in Reginald's place; he was necessary, he was the key, the password to this love.

But how splendid it would be if on his side Reginald had had the same weight, the same density. Whereas it was as she entered love that Nelly felt she became noble, strong, equal to anything, to joy, to death, it was as she returned to life that Reginald again became nobler, stronger, so that this couple which in the bedroom consisted of a peerless woman and an average man turned back, in the lights of the city, into a peerless man and a trivial woman . . . The transition took place when they embraced for the last time, exchanging their dignity. Did this mean that everything in life is incommensurate, that they would never be equals? Nelly sometimes told herself that there was a realm where this equality would take effect, but she did not encourage its advent, for she knew that it was the realm of Suffering.

It was precisely this fulfillment that informed Reginald. He was happy. As a matter of fact he had at first walked into a trap. To lure him out of that reticence he preferred in matters of love, it had taken precisely the hooks baited by Nelly. What she had fabricated to put herself on an equal footing with him was in fact precisely what Reginald desired: a married woman, but free and chaste; a free woman, but rich and independent, raised above easy loves and an easy life by a name, a dignity and a family situation of some consequence. From this he had fully benefited. The very secrecy of their love, that secret so carefully kept by Nelly because without it everything was lost, had seemed to Reginald a special kind of voluptuous satisfaction, almost the greatest of all. But for some time now he had been struck by this perfection, no longer by the external conditions of their passion, but by the passion itself. In Nelly's complexion, in her movements, her speech, there was a kind of beauty which seemed to lead this love even higher than he had supposed. Nelly gave him a sense of love as it is described and as it never is: an invincible power, a blind force, life itself. It was the only life this woman had; it was not possible that outside this passion she could live the limited and lamentable life of other women. It was the opposite of Psyche's story—this time it was the man who wanted to see love's face.

At first it was the same as in the story: he watched Nelly as she slept. But saw nothing: Nelly had two sleeps. Her sleep at home, her true sleep, from which she kept waking up, in which she cried out, dreamed, shuddered—when poor Gaston sometimes appeared as a corpse, sometimes as a ghost, sometimes with his trusting look, sometimes with an irritated expression he borrowed from Nelly's vague classical recollections of Nemesis—the sleep of someone who will be thirsty, get up, go back to sleep, betray herself, a sleep bordering on any villainy and any vice: she had not slept that sleep with Reginald. With him she slept a silent, dreamless sleep which left upon her only the signs of her happiness, of her incomparable tranquillity. Never caught out when she wakened, Nelly opened her eyes and smiled in calm and comfort. It was the sleep of a body which had never deceived, which had never deceived itself, and an awakening which knew it had nothing to fear from the day and its microscopes. This was the sleep she slept with Reginald, the sleep to which she surrendered herself confidently, for it gave her back a body which knew nothing, which was not aware of the problems of life, a pure body which suddenly became Nelly's body, Gaston's body, anybody's body once she crossed a certain frontier between the Rue Galilée and the Place de l'Etoile.

But it was this spectacle of Nelly in her second sleep, these truths of passion spread over this falsehood of skin and soul, which made Reginald reproach himself with being unworthy of her, which made him need to see Nelly not just in those few hours but as a woman perfect in all the circumstances and gestures of her day. Which led him, one afternoon, to follow her. Everything splendid a woman can create by ruse and deception a man soon demolishes by a thirst for perfection and with the help of truth and love . . . But also, who can suspect that a woman has two sleeps?

Instead of continuing in the car after dropping Nelly off near the Place des Etats-Unis, Reginald followed her, and indeed for a moment everything was just as it should have been. He had just dropped off a queen. She walked slowly, without glancing right or left, caressing only the children in the square who ran straight into her, like a queen. She was walking toward books, music, the exercise of some superior feminine function, perhaps a reception for the Papal Nuncio. Then came a sudden surprise. Her deliberation abandoned her, and her elevation: a gardener did not get out of her way, a few drops from his hose fell on hers —it was one of those gardeners who are instinctively more penetrating than the greatest psychologists, who had seen at once that Nelly was not a queen, who had seen what she really was, and who in his unconcern for her had been careless about three drops of water. That was nothing, yet that the elements and their behavior should show Nelly no respect rather shamed Reginald, it diminished her nobility . . . And that wasn't all! A butler out walking a poodle offered Nelly a remark which could not be the remark of a passer-by to a queen. And she almost fell, slipping on the sidewalk. All that world which, the moment he gave Nelly back to it, should have taken her with respect, received her like a gift, a reward—disdained her, insulted her! She looked much more like Cinderella returning to the jeers of her stepsisters than like that princess she really was. That what a man is a little tired of, what he has just enjoyed, turns out not to be the supreme nourishment of the rest of the world is always a disappointment. Then it wasn't a gift he was making to the universe by renouncing Nelly? Then it wasn't a gift he would receive when the universe restored her tomorrow at the usual time?

Moreover Nelly seemed neither to expect nor to demand homage in this realm. She existed here with a terrible egoism. Everything which, according to Reginald, was her dignity or her disgrace, seemed not to concern her. She looked at neither beggar nor child nor animal. There was nothing sovereign about her, all those defects and those particularities which attract the royal personnel in its divine false promenade toward the paralytic or the poodle or the bed of hortensias left Nelly quite indifferent. She inaugurated nothing. And indeed it was because she was nothing. That beauty Reginald saw in her when they were together in the apartment, that nobility, that lustre—it all seemed blurred, almost blotted out here. She was a woman, a pretty one, of course, but no murmur arose as she passed, the murmur Reginald was sure he would have to hear beside her. What was she like here—like a great lady? No. A trivial woman. She had suddenly returned to that category with which Reginald was not unfamiliar: the category of trivial women. Like them, she walked straight ahead, not strolling, not smiling. At any moment Reginald expected her to resume her other guise, expected her charm to return, her majesty, her incomparable style. Which did not happen at all. It seemed that by some mechanism her head must have been lowered a notch or two: there were constellations she could no longer see, the ones she had seen with Reginald.

Reginald was in anguish. Before his very eyes, and while he was still in love, was occurring that transformation which occurs only after love is over. Every man, when he is no longer in love, sees constellations rising that way, and sees the gaze of his former beloved sink to the horizon, and sees the vulgar world take back like a prize everything that his love now disdains, nose, neck, hands, everything in the body and the soul that was most cherished he now gives to a kind of open market where the exact price is ticketed, and he sometimes leaves just the eyes, or the mouth—some detail which he has given and she need not return. But Reginald was still in love, and it was not from him that the transformation was proceeding! There was a moment when Nelly, stopped by a streetcar, became herself again. "It's because she's thinking of me," Reginald decided, and as a matter of fact, she was thinking of him. No other variation. There seemed no reason to expect, as with other women, that Nelly would continue sinking in the class of women, or would suddenly rise again. She had stopped at this stage in a fashion which seemed eternal. She was a model of this genre.

Then a new kind of suffering began for Reginald, the converse of Gaston's: he realized that she was coming home. He saw her walk into a clockmaker's—here the watch was repaired which was not repaired near Reginald; into a laundry—here the sheets of the other establishment were washed; into a grocer's, a dry cleaner's—here spots were removed that Reginald had never seen. All that royal shopping she disdained in Reginald's neighborhood became the activity of a well-organized, serious little bourgeoise. And finally, when Nelly had utterly assumed her new appearance, someone came up to her, a little girl with a *pneumatique,* and Nelly's face changed, betrayed a relief which was also a vexation, for the *pneumatique* was from Helene

Guise, telling her that Gaston had been found. And the little girl was screaming. And Nelly made her be still. And everything a man could imagine at seeing his beloved panic-stricken by a *pneumatique* passed through Reginald's mind: her old lover was returning, her mother needed money. The lover she prefers to me has been killed in an automobile accident. Or her father the railway switchman has been bitten by a mad dog . . . He wasn't so wrong. It was something of the kind; it was worse; it was the fiancé who has found out that your son does not exist, and who wants to kill himself in order to die ahead of a horse that limped on its left hind leg, and who has learned that you have a lover, and that you love this lover who loves you too, well, to end the sentence, this fiancé had been found. The dénouement which occurs when this fiancé —who, and whom, and whose, and so on—is found is what will be disclosed in a moment. But Reginald, confronting this unexpected event, suddenly felt he was being indiscreet, and left off . . .

The luncheon was a long one. It was a luncheon of gourmets. They had to feed delicacies to bodies which seemed quite similar to bodies of the most ordinary sort. And the night was a long one. Here, however, it was different. Everything that was potentially beautiful in the night, its silence, its sounds, was on the contrary engulfed or extinguished in a child's heart, a heart which became that of a child all over again, a heart in which disappointment or pain or affliction, suddenly released from everything by which life had adulterated them, were as pure as in the nights of Reginald's childhood. If he had uttered a cry, it would have been a child's whimper. So little was his grief linked to the rest of the world's grief, so disengaged from the other sufferings of men, that it became a kind of gift. It had been a very long time since Reginald had known such pain, a pain that was all his own, a solo pain. War, deaths of parents and sons, the world's sadness and selfishness, his pain had nothing to do with them. It was so much the pain of innocence, of an immaculate age, an unharassed heart, that even while scarcely able to endure it, Reginald relished it, savored it again and again . . . And just as when he had been a little boy and in pain, so now Reginald instinctively glanced at his face in the mirror. He recoiled. That simple pain, that little boy's pain aged him incredibly.

A child's pains are for children. They are too terrible for grownups. Reginald's day was an agony. Everything in his usual life derided that magnificent life he had constructed outside of it. His luncheon, disdained for months, now retaliated on those sublime snacks taken apart from his real meals. Getting up at eight in the morning was implacable to getting up at seven in the evening. The same was true of all the actions of his day, of the most commonplace ones, before which their corresponding figures in the Other Life now bowed their head in shame. His tea mocked the other tea, his wine the other wine. All the most lamentable or the most charming persons he encountered took a merciless revenge on the person in that perfect life: they were true. The neighborhoods of Paris recovered their beauty, their superiority at the expense of this false neighborhood which had deceived him and which little by little destroyed itself. He discovered a whole series of things, of beings he had missed: girls, women's faces; he discovered them first in disparate fragments: a hand outside a car, a profile, a head in a shop, a foot on a curbstone; then all these separate parts combined to form, near the Place Vendôme, a whole woman, young, brilliant, whom he caught himself staring after and even following a few steps. A whole life triumphantly assailed him in all its lustre and loftiness to make him realize that he had forsaken it for what was mediocre, for what was trumpery—to make him realize that he was a fool.

From now on, it seemed to be telling him, let me choose my own nobility, my own degradation. Proud, fastidious, you have warded me off, and with me this magnificent creature, all to make a queen for yourself out of a trivial nonentity—surely you will no longer contest your stupidity and your clumsiness. And besides, your method is all wrong: if you try to take your revenge with this magnificent creature, look, she recognizes you, she smiles at you, and if you make her a queen too, if you love her apart from the world, she too will find a means of becoming trivial and mediocre all over again. That's what she's already becoming in your eyes, isn't she, as soon as you have imagined her, and she pales beside the next one, the new magnificent creature walking into the first shop, the real one, the only one, the one who will become, if you make her the queen of a kingdom cut off from your life, who will someday become a wretched creature like your Nelly. Incidentally, don't be angry with that Nelly of yours, she's not a liar, a woman's not a liar because she wears clothes given her by the man she loves. You simply cut them a little too sumptuous, sewed them a little too fine, my friend. We'll see, this afternoon, how you manage to return, now that you know, to the love story of the century, the love story of Nelly and Reginald. It's five o'clock, walk on to that extraordinary neighborhood of yours where they sell living sugar and miraculous tea, where socks grow on trees and a few fleas in the bed as well, as you'd discover if you spent the night there, go on and wait there, wait patiently for that paragon of nobility and virtue, wait for Nelly . . .

And Reginald began to talk to Nelly:

"Your lies, all right . . . I forgive them. Besides, I almost didn't hear: men almost don't listen. The timbre of a voice is enough to lead them, to reassure them. But it was everything which doesn't speak that I believed—I believed your body, always so noble among the petty gestures of love; I believed your eyes, always so lustrous with devotion; I believed your movements, always so terrible for the rest of humanity; most of all I believed the sound of your voice; you were lying in a clear, assured tone that was truth itself. That was why

I imagined a life of nobility under those magnificent appearances . . . You betrayed me. I am waiting for you."

He didn't have to wait long. Exactly on time, Nelly rang. Reginald opened the door. He wanted to open the door to a new woman whose very aspect would instantly confess everything, reveal everything, and he drew back, for he had opened the door to the old Nelly. In the darkness of the landing, then of the hall, the prelapsarian Nelly was created all over again without a single mistake, without a single regret. Her eyes were raised toward him, shining with joy. Her hands were raised toward him, as though dedicated. Everything the street had said about her face and her body was false: they were beautiful; people should have stopped and turned around when she passed. He opened the door to beauty, tenderness, devotion, to a kind of truth which so overwhelmed him that he did not understand it—which would have spared a lot of trouble—he did not see that it was love. He kissed her. He took her in his arms. He believed he was enjoying a pleasure of vengeance, an equivocal pleasure, kissing, embracing a trivial woman, a liar. He kissed Nelly's true lips, he embraced her true body, and he was honored by the kiss, by the embrace he received in return. He led her into the room, in front of the windows, wondering if the light would give her what he had not found, but the light on Nelly took away only the shadows, the light restored her to him in perfection.

They had their snack: tea, buttered toast, living

sugar, everything regained its advantage over its slanderous counterparts in the city. Nelly talked, Nelly undressed, Nelly went to bed. Everything from which Reginald expected avowal or betrayal, her gestures, her sighs, her clothes, offered him only confidence and calm. It was the scene of the little girl with the *pneumatique,* the scene of Nelly hysterical and almost vulgar which now became a lie, a dream. He lay down beside her, and here too his hypocritical research was frustrated: everything he asked of her in vulgarity or degradation she gave him back in honor. The setting sun glowed at the windows, cars drove through the secluded street, a breeze stirred the curtains. The nobility of the place and of the hour were not contradicted even for a second. Yes, he felt it—all he needed to do was not leave, not get up, merely spend the rest of his life in this room, in this hour, for everything to be supremely true. And she had fallen asleep now. And he had to waken her, for it was late. Reginald was seized by fear, by pity, for her sudden waking would be that of a sleepwalker. If he wakened her abruptly, she would call out another name, ask for other clothes. He shook her. As you shake someone who must catch a train, who has received a special delivery letter.

But none of this agitation troubled Nelly. She wakened as she always wakened. Under Reginald's hands, which held her wrists as though at the end of a struggle, she did not confuse her anguish with her joy, her Parisienne's chic with her beauty as a living woman.

Through her still-closed eyes she saw everything—the magnificent sunset, and the life lovers have, and Reginald kneeling beside her as though beside a grave being opened, she saw him kneeling there, soon, beside her own grave . . . And his name? Was her own name Nelly? She smiled and fell asleep again. Almost in tears, one knee raised, like the Angel of the Last Judgment about to tell a woman who believes she is innocent that she is damned, Reginald watched and waited, suddenly conscious that all the lies, at one stroke, were on his side now.

And then occurred the same separation. Not at the same point. She asked him to drop her near the Place de la Concorde. Here, again, Reginald got out of the car and followed her. He would see what became of her. Had she vulgarized and diminished herself only because she had entered her private circle? Perhaps she assumed her trivial aspect only in this milieu of family worries, of domestic cares. Perhaps everywhere else, here, in this magnificent square where everything turned into luxury and grandeur, and there toward the Seine and the Louvre, and there toward the gardens, she would remain herself . . . But he had to admit she did not. In the Place where Louis XVI had regained his grandeur, despite recent historical events and the traces of bullets on the walls of the Crillon, he saw how the old tranquil Nelly suddenly turned into a troubled woman, walked more stiffly, he could not quite see her face, but he could guess from her hair, her hair seemed more determined. Her face grew dry, hard. And her worries were practical ones; in front of the shop windows she no longer stopped only for objects which attract great souls. Her beauty, too, diminished. Not so much that a man didn't try to speak to her. She put him in his place. A great soul does not put such persons in their place, a great soul dismisses them with a smile, a glance, a silence. Nelly put the man in his place like a woman accustomed to putting men in their place.

What if he caught up with her, Reginald wondered . . . Would his presence in the middle of this very street restore to Nelly what had so pitilessly abandoned her?

He caught up with her. Doubtless she would be troubled, overtaken like this in *flagrante delicto,* stark naked with her life which turned out to be so ordinary. He touched her shoulder. But among all the touches which Paris and the world could give her, Nelly knew the touch of her lover's hand. She offered him the face of that afternoon, she regained her beauty, her tranquillity returned. He took her arm, he stopped her with some excuse; everything had that marvelous quality, that pure, true color. People stopped to glance at this couple, suddenly formed anew. He left her . . .

So it was true! My God, what a pathetic revelation! All of Nelly's splendor came from him! Nelly became the real Nelly only with him, for him. Upon discovering that he was a principle of elevation, of beauty, a profound disappointment overwhelmed Reginald. It brought him back to himself, only to himself.

If all that glory which a new life had afforded him for five months, if that disclosure of love, of woman, was merely an impulse of his own, merely a kind of suggestion exercised upon an average little Parisienne—if that was all! Then it was no longer that accession of youth, of instinctive strength, that union of two equal beings, but a kind of old age, a combination between forty, or wisdom, and twenty, or folly, which created—but chimerically, *à la* Faust—this perfect couple. Tears filled his eyes. Reginald did not want to give. He wanted to receive. Is there a worse despair than to believe you are under an obligation and to discover you are a benefactor?

He tried not to be one. During their next times together he arrived cross, stubborn. Uncertain what he would do, hesitant to acknowledge his own feelings, he became nervous, brutal. But he had to admit that the aura which enveloped Nelly did not come only from his gestures, from his appearance. She remained the same under this limelight of nerves and harshness, astonished only as much as the real Nelly would seem to be astonished, soothing him, solicitous . . . Nelly's splendor was no second-rate mimicry. It came from a deeper source. But it was not comfort to know he was a purifier at heart.

Then, for a whole week, he could not help making her lie. He forced her to talk about those places she had never been. It was incredible how she managed to dissimulate and to embellish what Reginald gradually learned from her. You would never have said it was a lie. You would have said it was a kind of modesty. Lightly, and with the skill and the instinct of a Vestal, by an inspired impulse of invention, she veiled what her life had to conceal. So that sometimes Reginald had the impression that this existence Nelly dissimulated commanded her no more than Original Sin commands a woman. It was just as theoretical, just as remote; Original Sin has a hypothesis of vulgarity about it, a certain desiccation, whereas this sin of lying liberated Nelly, leaving her real life in a dazzling truth. It was all becoming a game Reginald was losing, especially since jealousy was not far off . . . He still contained it. He tried to remind himself that after all Nelly was free to do as she liked; he cast about in vain for the promises she had made him, the reassurances, and anxiously discovered that this woman whom he believed to be the only woman in the world had never said she loved only him, had never said only Reginald was her lover, had never claimed she did not live with another man, with two other men, with all other men. This woman who was made for Reginald had never told him she wasn't made for everyone else as well. On this point there had been no lie. She had never severed herself from all that is terrible in life: she had never said she did not have a tyrannical mother, a ridiculous lover, an impecunious and mediocre existence. He tried—by coaxing, by laying traps into which any other woman would have fallen in a moment of enthusiasm or an inability to contain herself—he tried to make her say she lived only for him, only with him. He never succeeded. She seemed to know nothing about her other life, but she could not compromise herself in its regard. She simply treated the present the way so many other lovers treat the future: with a tacit reserve. How many times he was tempted to betray himself, to tell her he knew everything. But he always stopped in time, in a kind of pity, the pity you take on a sleepwalker before shouting out her name.

11

Nelly, for her part, had certainly noticed a change in Reginald's spirits. But she was not worried by the change at first—quite the contrary. She interpreted it as a favorable development in Reginald's nature and in his love. She was not sorry that he finally showed irritability, dissatisfaction, anxiety. A god and a goddess in love with each other is all very well, but perfection sustains them in an immobility which is anything but desirable for human beings. The fact that Reginald consented to abandon that ambrosial atmosphere was a relief, a sign of life. It was also a promise: it meant that like other irritable and active men, he would get down from his pedestal, take an interest in her. She, too, had the impression sometimes of being touched, of being loved only by means of a double, through an envelope which gave such love a certain nobility but also a certain studied non-existence. That peevish voice reached her real ears, those blazing eyes, her real eyes.

Once outside the Olympian and insensitive zones which so deceptively resemble Olympian and selfish ones, Reginald would perhaps discover at last that the strongest and most apparently satisfied woman needs the same help and support as the weakest. There was some slight chance she might find at last a realm with a new order, an unclassifiable order, of preoccupations and pleasures. For between this happy ataraxia of life with Reginald and that arid countenance of life with Gaston, between this plenitude and that vital egoism, to both of which she could assign the proper sentiments, for she had hitherto revealed only the superior order of sentiments —generosity, devotion, utter joy—and their inferior order, Nelly felt the gradual onset of another order which she had not suspected until now, and for which she found no realm. This was the realm in which she might burst into tears for no reason, or suffer the emotions of a naive child because the sun rose or because it set, the realm of a liaison between all her limbs, all her faculties, and certain figures she had quite disdained hitherto, a liaison with spring, a liaison with summer, a liaison with the stars in general, or in particular. There was suddenly something inside her, something quite small but very specific and very sensitive, linked to all abstractions and all entities. And she suffered each time she was made aware of those links, for she did not understand the object of this new emotion, and she could not accommodate it in her day. It was a kind of second secret she had vis-à-vis Reginald, a secret which seemed more serious than the other one, for it had come into being since she knew him. There could be no question of having a third lover for this third heart.

So if Reginald agreed to step down from that pedestal on which they both, once a day, performed the *tableau vivant* of dignity and love, perhaps he would help her that way. Each impatience Reginald showed, each criticism Reginald made, seemed a promise of that stopover, of that sojourn in a country where she would no longer be, in Reginald's arms, that statue she forced herself to keep young and smiling, but a mass of flesh and blood, of trust, of avowal. Already, when she wakened in the night—for she continually wakened with a start out of her true sleep—she imagined Reginald beside her, the angry, suspicious, irritable Reginald, and she called that Sleeping With Reginald; and, with this mannequin stretched out beside her now, the curious something inside her attached itself to everything it could: to cockcrow, to twilight, to childhood memories. And in this delighted glimpse, between her two other lives, of a realm of relaxation, of emotion, which so enriched her, Nelly lied to Reginald more joyously than ever. She was inspired to speak of her old husband, of his first cars. It all came so easily: the names of his horses, the names of his Hungarian aunts. Until that day when she saw in Reginald's eyes a look there was no mistaking, a look of pain, of resentment, of torment which left no doubt: he knew everything.

Nelly was brave. She did not move. It had come almost at the beginning of their two hours, at the moment when they usually went to bed. She was overcome by an uncoercible fear, the fear she might have felt some night at seeing a robber's feet sticking out from under the bed. But she behaved as she would have behaved in that eventuality. She responded to Reginald's trap by entering it all the more readily; she embroidered on the old Hungarian grandmother with whom she used to listen to *La Vie Parisienne* on the radio; she continued undressing that body, sacred a moment ago, the body of a princess, and now no longer anything but a trivial woman's body. Around it she made, though she felt it had been dethroned, vanquished, all the habitual gestures. It was the first time she had undressed, in front of Reginald, the body which belonged to Gaston, the first time she had been forced into that mortification. The throat, the arms, the nape of the neck which belonged to Gaston, then the legs—she revealed them with a false nonchalance but with an intense pain which nearly made her cry out. It was hideous, that grin on Reginald's face, those sarcastic comments of Reginald's, that dreadful counter-lie alongside the real lie which asked today, as it had asked yesterday, only to become a tender and indisputable truth. Did he know about Gaston? Did he know about the other two? Did this body also belong to Hervé? To poor Jacques? Jacques at least had been killed in a car crash. They said he had been ogling a pretty girl on the outskirts of Dijon and hadn't seen the Paris-Pontarlier bus. Death had come from Pontarlier at less than fifty kilometers an hour. At least Jacques, by dying, had given up his rights. If Gaston were dead, he would have given them up too. How could she think of such a thing! My God, if she could just get all that out of her mind! If only—just now, when he was about to take her in his arms—she didn't remember that her body had been Gaston's, or Hervé's! Did he see there was no blood left in her veins? The only way of escaping this nightmare was to imagine Reginald was someone else, the fourth—there would never be a fourth, but she had to imagine it—and to imagine him jealous, and to think that she was giving him the body that belonged to Reginald. She closed her eyes. She suffered terrible pain embracing a Reginald who was no longer Reginald, giving herself to another man, but at least she was giving him the woman who belonged to Reginald.

That was how a week passed: still no news of Gaston. People supposed he had left for America. The jewels he must have ordered for their engagement were beginning to arrive. He had forgotten to cancel the order. A square diamond arrived, a barrette, and a gold-and-diamond pendant on which, when you breathed on it, you could read *Gaston & Nelly*. If he had ordered the flowers in advance, with his methodical mind, they would be coming soon.

As for Reginald, he didn't seem to know just what he was going to do. Sometimes she felt he was ready to submit, to change this extraordinary love into a charming episode. Sometimes he seemed horribly annoyed to be tricked this way—to let himself be tricked. Sometimes, on the other hand, she felt how much he pitied her. She had to be very strong then, not to tell everything. But she resisted because she did not believe herself, because she did not want to be pitied. She persisted in believing she was enviable, privileged. To give in, to burst into tears and confess in Reginald's arms, to avow her true love, was all very well, and might have been very comforting, and might also have been the means of acquiring Reginald. But it was an abdication. There was a kind of power over life which she did not intend to renounce, a creation of life which she would pursue to the end, even under the eyes of those who knew the truth. Under the horror-stricken eyes of Reginald, she denied with every word, with every gesture, the obvious. She insisted on certain lies. Not in order to anger him, to provoke an outburst, but in order to keep at her side her invented world, out of loyalty, an accomplice's loyalty to all the other accomplices. Her conscience, moreover, was clear. She felt guilty of nothing with Reginald. She was at ease with him. The only painful moment, the moment when Reginald thought she belonged to other men, she had rendered harmless, for herself, by her recipe: he was a new lover, a woman's memory does not extend beyond the last lover, and this last lover was Reginald. This body impervious to the past bore no imprint, no memory but Reginald's. She was proud to disclose, to denude, to display the body which belonged to Reginald.

But Reginald, who was not informed of this recipe for virginity, took her ostentation for a new lie, almost for provocation. He suffered. Which did no harm. Nelly was relieved by such suffering, and she did not try to remedy it—on the contrary. She carried her cruelty to the point of introducing real lies between them, the lies of other women, telling him she had been to a certain concert and then getting the details mixed up; paving their afternoon with lies which Reginald listened to in horror; especially since Nelly, in the supremacy of her truth, was radiant with a beauty, a tranquillity, a sincerity which must have stirred in Reginald's memory every line of poetry, every maxim he had ever heard about women bewitched, women possessed, demon women . . . Until the day when, perhaps warned by one of Nelly's exaggerations, he understood; he understood that Nelly knew he knew. And Nelly, too, saw at the same moment that he understood.

There was suddenly an anguish in the room which could not be mistaken: the anguish which precedes separations, departures, deaths. These two human beings were looking at each other the way two beings never see each other, in one of those flashes when everything is revealed: face to face, so that the eyes are forever singed by such a confrontation. But Nelly, inexperienced though she was, understood the situation better than Reginald. She understood that there are two kinds of separation: the kind which is necessary and the kind which is artificial, not fatal, not indispensable, but brought about by a kind of feeble destiny which, in its impotence, enforces the gestures of separation, makes the responsibility for separation fall on human beings. Which was exactly the present case. If Reginald and

Nelly went on with their vain and artificial combat, they would have to separate. That was the anything but ineluctable denouement one comes to in the world and in tragedies. To satisfy such a destiny, to give everything a more fatal quality, they must say nothing, they must go on with their afternoon, they must part as usual, one of them must say "until tomorrow" and the other must answer "tomorrow" and they must never see each other again. Human beings are stupid enough to execute on their own the plans of a second-rate destiny.

Nelly did not want it to be this way. Till now, she had made her own destiny. And Reginald, for his part, suspected something too. He saw Nelly suddenly splendid and suddenly disarmed, suddenly above every law and exposed to every pain. She seemed to him, even after he had suffered so much from her lies, less a liar than the suddenly betrayed ally of a human life antagonistic to habitual life, a transgressor only a mechanical and theoretical justice could condemn. He had an impulse to take her in his arms, he realized her love, he realized that on no important point had she lied to him: she loved him more than anything in the world, she was the only woman in the world for him, the two of them formed the only couple . . . He realized vaguely that at this altitude, in this quite unpopulated realm, there were no rules to follow; that there was only, for example, a magnificent precedent of kneeling before the lying woman, of embracing the lying woman, of proposing to the lying woman, a precedent to be set for the future of mankind. But he did not realize everything. He failed to see in Nelly's sudden efflorescence, in that pride by which she was suddenly illuminated, what was really there: the arrival in that realm where everything is indifferent to you if it is not devotion and love, an approach, as advanced as an approach can be, to all the recourses of love, including death—he did not see on Nelly's body the reflection of all those dangers and all those beauties amid which she finally understood herself—and perhaps him as well—but only a kind of ostentation which rejected everything he thought he offered—though he offered nothing but passion and jealousy—a provocation which rejected forgiveness and pity. That was why, as he left, he said to her: "Until tomorrow."

That was why she answered: "Tomorrow."

And why they never saw each other again.

12

If Nelly had never felt inferior to this world, for which she had neither admiration nor consideration, it was because she had three or four resources against it. The first was Reginald, had been Reginald for two years. The second was Stalin. The third was Fontranges. It is evident that she did not pick them out of a hat. But that an average soul should take such stars for lodestones was not a bad sign either. What she had asked of Reginald we now know. What she would ask of Stalin she did not yet know herself, but she could not get rid of the idea that if she ever addressed herself to this man above all other men, he would avenge her. Stalin would avenge her for indignities, for conspiracies, for poverty. The moment had not yet come. And lastly there was that amazing man she had heard about from Eglantine, the man named Fontranges. Like some animal which when stung or sick immediately seeks out the antidote herb—it was not Stalin this time: Stalin could do nothing to reunite a heart with a heart which fled it—Nelly, leaving Reginald, went looking for Fontranges.

She went looking for him the way she would have looked for Stalin, to avenge herself on mediocrity, on cowardice, on compromise. She had to find some recourse—against what? When she tried to clarify her thoughts, it was against a kind of false virtue, of prejudice, or rather against those who lack imagination, against life itself, insofar as life lacked imagination. The comparison was rather disadvantageous for Fontranges, but she went looking for him the way the little heroine flouted by life goes looking for Charlie Chaplin . . .

She had glimpsed Fontranges. She knew the story of his son, and the story of his horse Sheba, and the story of Eglantine. Everything she tried to see in the theatre, everything she tried to read made her suffer, sounded false to her, the way music can sound false. Those stories of Werther, of Manon: pathetic. That there was no means to cancel the commitments life makes for you without your consent, that it was impossible to deny the past—this led Nelly to doubt her qualifications for life. Who could justify her in her own eyes? Her mother? Her mother reprimanded her for Gaston's disappearance as if Nelly had impounded him. The "scum"? Ordinary people by whom she supposed herself understood and admired? Not at all. The "scum" betrayed her. The sweepers and street sprinklers noticed her two or three seconds later than usual, so that she was touched by a dust of detritus, a dew of spray. Road workers, instead of using friendly words appreciated Nelly flatteringly but brutally. One day she stepped into a bus with a kind of confidence in what is not rich, not warped, not selfish, with a sudden disgust for taxis and private cars: here everyone conspired against her; she was treated not only as an intruder but as an undesirable by the conductress, in league with a bakery saleswoman and a little old gentleman.

Then came the day when she had to run the gauntlet, actually, of the "scum," when she had to take a taxi to Mantes the first afternoon of the six-day bicycle races. This was a disaster. They were all there, lined up as she passed. She recognized the boys in red scarves, in purple jerseys, in yellow-and-green-striped jerseys, and their girls, the ones with whom she usually gossiped, and the faces of the workmen she had met on the day of municipal elections, and their wives whose scrofulous children she had caressed out of self-indulgence and also the way queens caress the scrofulous, with the certainty of curing them. And everyone, lined up almost at attention along her route, behaved toward Nelly, who had imagined she was reviewing the millions of Parisians she assumed won over to her cause, like insurgent soldiers toward a general who still believes in the noble sentiments of the troops and has decided to tour their sector. Was it on account of the little Second Empire hat she was wearing that they threw wadded-up newspapers which hit her in the face, so that for a kilometer she was obliged to close the window against which the newspapers battered? No, it was because they saw Nelly alone, it was because they saw Nelly sad, because they felt she needed help, the help of precisely the million men they constituted. A ten-minute target for all the cowardice and ridicule of men, Nelly would have been reduced to tears without the presence of the old driver who never spoke a word, not even flinching when a newspaper happened to hit him. "They're lively" was all he said, when they reached Mantes. He had been able to see the liveliness in those faces of demons and acid throwers. At home, too, moreover, tradesmen had begun the attack. Little Lulu came back in a rage from the grocery or the bistro where she had struggled for Madame, who was not at all Madame, the house painters said, but Mademoiselle. And you know what that means.

"She is too Madame," Lulu said, ready to burst.

The house painters winked at the plasterers. "Are there many Monsieurs who come to see your Madame?"

Poor Lulu fell into the trap. "Yes, there are. Many. And they're a lot better looking than you are. You get paint and plaster all over everything."

"Do they take off Madame's paint?"

Lulu began to guess that this was shaky ground. "What paint?"

"You know, do they kiss her?"

Lulu felt rebellion seize her. She mustered everything she thought was hardest, meanest in herself: it was only what was purest. With all this impulse of unconscious purity, she thought of her beloved Madame. Which is to say that she saw Madame as a miracle of purity, someone these filthy men could never touch, someone only white hands could touch, but white from inside, not the plasterers'—above all, someone whose compromises she did not even suspect, though she saw their menacing shadow on the horizon. "Kiss Madame? Never."

"You just didn't see."

Then she lied. "Yes, I saw. I saw them come, one Monsieur after another. But they're very nice, very polite, not like you. They're invited. They have to be invited. Anyone who came without being invited would be shown the door."

They had only to try.

"Don't you think they kiss her, just because they're invited?"

"No, they don't kiss her. I know for sure. When Madame is alone with a Monsieur, I watch through the keyhole. They sit in two chairs and talk on opposite sides of the room. Or she plays the piano and he listens. And I see it all. Or she makes him tea, and he couldn't kiss her with a cup in his hand."

"Watch them when they come home from the theatre."

"They do kiss her hand . . . Besides, everyone knows what a woman is if she lets herself be kissed."

A laugh swept through the bistro. The plasterer took Lulu in his arms and kissed her despite her struggles. He smelled of red wine. It is terrible to be kissed. No, it wasn't possible. Madame had never let herself be kissed! She told Madame everything, kissing her. Oh how nice it was being kissed by Madame!

What did Nelly want, trying to find Fontranges? She didn't really know. But she had the impression that near Fontranges she would be closer to her own kind. This man who had never lied—except once, on the very day when Nelly happened to be at Saint-Cloud, the day they were going to shoot his mare because they thought her leg was broken, and Fontranges, caressing his mare that understood everything, told her she would be all right, told her she would be back on her feet in no time, would catch up with the others, would win the race—Fontranges who had never made a duplicitous gesture, never entertained a suspect thought, why was it that Nelly felt he was not only her one ally but her one relative, though she was a lying woman who lived a double life?

She and Eglantine had followed Fontranges—they had come to Saint-Cloud precisely to watch Sheba's filly run, and they had not been able to contain themselves, they had hurried to the track where the jockey in Fontranges' colors was marking the place Tamar had fallen in ruby silks. Fontranges bent down over the mare—not too far, for she had raised her head when she heard him approach . . . Each one, man and beast, had come halfway, as usual, and Fontranges, Fontranges' mouth which no lie had ever touched, said to Tamar what Nelly herself would have said: that she would be all right, that she would go back to Nogent-sur-Seine, that she would soon be in her own pasture, far from races organized by men. And the mare, though Eglantine had tears in her eyes, believed everything, and then there occurred that little miracle which made Tamar's leg suddenly all right, even though the veterinary was standing right there with his revolver.

It will be said that there are too many horses in this story, but the fact is that they turn up quite naturally. A man on horseback no longer needs to lie. An equestrian Nelly felt equal at last to all that truth she so rarely touched on foot. This was Fontranges' opinion, when so many squadrons of hussars and dragoons were suppressed; cavalry regiments were so many truths in relation to infantry regiments, however real, or in relation to aviation squadrons, however whimsical. So when he had decided not to run Tamar in any more races, and when Eglantine said she never rode, Fontranges gave her to Nelly and asked if she would ride the mare in the Bois. Thus elevated, Nelly found herself in an atmosphere where lies no longer existed. But that was not the only reason that she went on seeing Fontranges, that they met on foot every day. She did not know just why, but she followed Fontranges the way you follow someone who has a key.

Autumn was coming. Autumn too seemed to have a key. Never had Nelly known a season which seemed to understand so much, to explain so much. Nelly was rather frightened by nature. Her life had kept her quite far from it. She entertained toward this soft and bushy appearance the same apprehension as the pilot over a virgin forest: what seems a caress for the plane would be a hideous death. But at a distance, those trees in the Bois she had never approached, those meadows on which she had been too delicately dressed, too starched to sit, those pools across which a spirit of poetic prudery had forbidden her to canoe, at a distance she let her mind be caressed by them. The setting of the same sun she hated seeing rise filled the sky with that scarlet which heralds war to nations but to Nelly heralded a kind of peace with herself. It also seemed that if she could discover how this autumn differed from the usual seasons, she would discover a clue, a hint of how to live her life.

From Gaston, no news. From Reginald, nothing. These two men who lived only for Nelly, who spent no moment without evoking her, when they were not actually touching her, and who had made such an uproar in creation on her account—it had been enough for some screw in their brain to turn a single thread for them to disappear, for them to have never existed. She, she might be a lying woman, but she was more faithful than that. She did not believe in the impossible, she did not believe in the apparent, she still believed in a mild and enslaved Gaston, whereas everything proved he was rebellious and full of hate, she still believed in a trusting and indestructible Reginald, whereas everything proved he was incredulous and devastated. She suffered from their absence as though it were not an absence but a metempsychosis, as though they had assumed another form, as though they had both been changed—if not into a tree or a bird, then into another

Gaston, another Reginald whom some magic word would restore to what they had once been.

As for Gaston, moreover, she had made up her mind. She felt friendship for him, pity, sometimes a vestige of old and intimate habits; but she felt he was indispensable to her only insofar as you need to pity someone. She merely regretted that he had assumed the form of a hostile Gaston. In the very variety of Gastons, there were so many models he might have chosen, so many kinder, more reasonable models. Among the plants on her terrace, there was a certain succulent she could not look at without thinking of Gaston. It was this plant Gaston must have become, must have turned himself into . . . It was a succulent, an ordinary one, with something loyal, trusting about it, and a few huge spines which sometimes pricked you but which were easy to remove, not at all like cactus spines. It absorbed the water she gave it greedily, rapidly, the way Gaston drank his vermouth. Afterwards, it seemed to wheeze and puff like Gaston. It did not speak, rather like Gaston. Was she being unfaithful to Reginald by having, in this gentle and primitive form, a friend who had chosen a spiteful form only out of naiveté and by mistake? It was in fact the only form in which Nelly could really love and bear Gaston, this funerary urn whose ashes were sap, that pure sap which keeps you from dying of thirst in the desert. From time to time a branch yellowed, reddened; Nelly tried to save it by pruning, spraying, heat; she washed the leaves with milk, according to the advice of a Moroccan. That was all she could do for Gaston. She was even surprised to discover she felt that much friendship for Gaston. The succulent taught her. She really singled it out among the succulents, or among the desiccants, for that matter, and when an accident caused by Lulu broke off the finest leaf, she suffered a regret less evident but more profound than if Gaston himself had broken an arm or a leg. That was how Nelly realized that there had been a conflict between Gaston and Reginald.

In Reginald's case, she decided he was Tamar. Everything concurred to prove it. Ever since Tamar had appeared, Reginald had no longer existed. She had heard Reginald's last words, "until tomorrow" a few hours before learning of Tamar's existence. That a famous statesman should suddenly change into a three-year-old filly was of course no everyday occurrence; it was an odd precedent. It took Nelly's eye to recognize Reginald's legs, Reginald's shoulders, in the legs and shoulders of Tamar. Tamar's lashes, too, were longer. The velvety place where you kissed Tamar was softer than any place on Reginald. But he had obviously wanted to profit by such advantages. He had become a mare out of sweetness, he had chosen the opposite sex out of tenderness; it mattered little enough from a certain point of view, since chastity was imposed upon Tamar, but it did prove, on Reginald's part, a desire to humiliate himself—it was an admission.

The newspapers still mentioned Reginald, described his endeavors, his inspired interpellations in the Chamber of Deputies: that was because he turned into Tamar only during the hours when he used to meet Nelly. And Nelly rode Tamar only during those hours. And in spite of all the pain it caused to find Tamar whinnying instead of speaking, turning her rump instead of opening her arms, nonetheless riding Tamar bareback you felt that she understood you, that she liked carrying you, and that she made certain gestures which suggested Reginald: she tossed her head the way Reginald sometimes did, and there were those moments of silence when Tamar, standing in front of the Cucufa Pond or the rifle range, watched and listened in a way that was incredibly reminiscent of Reginald leaning on the windowsill and watching the sunset through the sock hanging in the tree. Tamar did not quite understand when Nelly talked to her on their rides, told her everything: that she loved only Tamar, that she would kill herself if Tamar didn't change back into a man some day, that she mustn't wait too long, for horses age faster than men, that the story of the poor succulent was a thing of the past, that even if Nelly found the magic word to transform the succulent into Gaston, she would arrange matters so as to forget it. And Tamar would stop, turn her head, scrape her hoof on the ground, vaguely understanding something, a gentle language without specific meaning, something like: Tamar aoli remeninovelibacoreginaldipaloliebala-tracmeoselpafiertetamar . . . And that meant a good deal; but, suddenly conscious of the metamorphosis of which she was the object, Tamar chose the first excuse to bolt, glancing back under her mocking lashes at a surprised Nelly, then galloping until the moment when an encounter with another horse stopped her, shook her from head to foot, so that the shock rose up into Nelly and aroused memories which brought tears to her eyes.

Fontranges saw those tears. He stopped. He stared at the tears with that same respect he had for water, for dew, for everything which fertilizes. Nelly was crying hard now: for days she had felt she was going to cry and she had worn no mascara on her eyes, no rouge on her cheeks. Down to her lips, there was nothing to fear from tears.

"Why are you crying?"

Sheba and Tamar had stopped and were gently nibbling each other: you cannot take too much advantage of human tears—human beings weep so seldom.

"I used to have two friends. One has become a succulent and the other has become Tamar . . ."

Fontranges was not a man for whom such language was incomprehensible. "And you don't know the magic word which will turn them back?"

"No. I've lost it."

"Was it their own fault they were changed, or someone else's?"

"No. Mine."

"Then the word doesn't exist yet. You have to invent it. Which is very difficult. Are you sure there wasn't a word? What did you say the last time you saw them?"

Nelly remembered very well. "I said to the first one: 'What's the matter with you, Gaston?' "

"What kind of succulent is it?"

"I'm not sure."

"Then we'll have to have a look. I know a specialist in succulents . . . And what did you say to Tamar?"

"I said 'tomorrow.' "

Fontranges must have known that mares don't turn back into men easily, for he seemed less assured about the friend changed into Tamar than about the friend changed into a succulent. He must have had some experience concerning the friendships of men and horses which had not given him complete confidence. But his face was so imbued with sympathy for Nelly that it seemed imbued with interest in the problem. He was looking for the means of making this woman happy. He was looking for happiness. But he seemed to be looking for the word, a word. Nelly stared at him as if, by a word, he was about to find the secret of happiness. Until Tamar, shying, reared up on her hind legs in an impulse which startled both Nelly and Fontranges, an impulse to resume her former posture . . . Nelly gently convinced her to remain a quadruped. And they resumed their ride.

"Did you love them both?" Fontranges asked.

"No. Only one. I love only one. But that didn't stop me from turning the other into a succulent."

"Don't confuse matters. If you love only one of the two, why bother about the other?"

"Because he sacrificed everything for me, and because I lied to him."

It was curious to see how Fontranges' presence encouraged both precision and generosity. Nelly was beginning to understand herself, to understand words too.

"And the other one? Doesn't he love you any more?"

"I think he still loves me. But I lied to him."

"Do you really believe in lying?"

What did he mean? Did he mean that lying is a speech defect which has to be interpreted? Did he mean that everything is the truth? Oh my God, was he going to find the real word: that lying is all that has been created by man against a creation implacable to truth!

"Men no longer say what they mean very clearly," Fontranges said. "Yesterday, for example, I was in a café called The English Bar. There were records playing. Either a song called *The Busy Bee* or another one called *The Girl Friend*. I was trying to figure out which one was playing. I imagined I would guess immediately whether the music was about a busy bee or a girl friend . . . But it was impossible. Even though there are differences between them. One flies, sucks, stings. The other smiles, dances, kisses. One alights, quivers, hums. The other sits down, dreams, sings. Now it was really impossible to tell if the composer was dealing with the bee or the girl. It seems to me that from the very first note, if I had been the composer, the whole truth would have come out. Nothing of the kind. As a matter of fact, as far as I could tell, everything the composer of the bee had written could just as well apply to the girl friend, and vice versa. For in the long run the one works, buzzes, sleeps at night. The other listens to what you can't hear, says nothing, waits at her window. Even so, maybe it's just as well that *The Busy Bee* and *The Girl Friend* aren't so different after all: the one glitters in the sun, loves flowers, dies at night; the other loves flowers and is glittering, and mortal. But I suppose the same perplexity would come up between the friend changed into a succulent and the Bishop of Montélimar. Our means of expression are limited. Hence lying."

Nelly was thinking about the difference between the symphony of the truthful girl and the symphony of the lying woman. Obviously the truth requires brasses, but so does a brazen lie. That way men can tell where they are, for men understand nothing. But God, Who understands everything, is deceived.

"God," Fontranges said.

By what reasoning had Fontranges been led to God? Nelly doubted that it was the same as hers. He must have reached God by following his story of *The Busy Bee* and *The Girl Friend* to its logical conclusion. But in any case, there they both were.

"God," Fontranges said, "has given each of us the means of being his own hero. We have no life—what is fifty or eighty years on earth? But each of us can exist if he has his legendary existence. The man or woman who is not legendary is nothing. It's all a matter of finding your legend."

Nelly was thinking that she had had an idea like

that once, the day she discovered that there were people who had their song and people who had none. The day she was searching for the grace which would give each of her words that legendary aspect and tone, when she was trying to see if the story of her life might be read aloud by some student with a husky and tentative voice out of some book like the Golden Legend. So many saints in the Golden Legend had only simple lives, ordinary lives, into which the legendary was introduced only by a kind of tenderness and naiveté of style. If a tender and naive writer took Nelly's life, could he manage to make it into one of those gold-framed chapters with sufferings and martyrdoms in the middle? Wasn't Nelly's suffering greater than that of the martyrs who had been burned at the stake or eaten by lions, since they were glad to suffer and she was not? Wasn't Nelly the true martyr? There had been a saint with an ivy bush, a saint with a goldfinch, a saint with a smile—why not a saint with a lie? . . . Nelly imagined the story of her life as told by Fontranges. She would have liked to hear him recite it aloud, not ennobling its actions—some of which she admitted were suspect—but lending them, by epic or narrative devices, that breadth which, by emphasizing them, justifies them. She wanted to encourage him, she said: "There are many actions in my life which seem to me not to fit your theory."

Tamar was enjoying her dignity as a mare. She pranced where she stood, without trying to move on. She pranced in the legend of Tamar.

"Are you so sure of that? Do you think, at your age, that you can already judge your actions? You see me as I am today, quite calm, quite happy. That's because I've only just come to understand what I've always regarded as the crime of my youth. You're looking at a man whose remorse has suddenly become a jubilation. My mother died when I was eight. They took her to the sanitarium, I promised to write her every day, I cried, I struggled, I hung onto the stretcher, for they told me not to touch her, then to her blanket which came away in my hands, so that she lay all uncovered with her bare arms that she dared not hold out to me for she knew I would never let them go again, then to the strap of the stretcher, then to the door of the carriage, then to the horses. They dragged me away sobbing, and I spent the first three days writing endless letters in which I implored her to get well, in which I embraced her; and she apparently kept the last letter in her bed, putting the first two in a box she had bought on purpose, and even numbering them. And on the fourth day, a Belgian griffon arrived at the gamekeeper's, and I spent the day with the Belgian griffon, not writing any letter. And on the fifth day I got up at six in the morning to go see my Belgian griffon, which had adopted me, which obeyed no one but me. And on the sixth day, I received a telegram from my father telling me that my mother was worse, that I must write her. And I spent that sixth day with the Belgian griffon, and when I went home to write the letter I was tired, I fell asleep, I dreamed about the Belgian griffon. And on the seventh day my mother died. And they took me by train to Paris, and I was led to her bedside. Her hands were folded over my third letter. And the box was still on the table, only it was missing the four letters that would have eased her death. And ever since then I have written those missing letters—even when I was grown up, I wrote them over and over. And remorse for that ingratitude of mine has tormented most of my nights until one morning the old butler told me that my mother knew I didn't have time to write her on account of a Belgian griffon. She knew I would come, that smile was for me; she didn't have any grudge against the Belgian griffon. She had said: 'I'm glad the boy likes dogs.' I didn't know any of that, but she had understood my life needed that little crime in it to give it a quality, to give it a style right at the start. After that I didn't pet the griffon again. I had vowed never to speak to it again, never to visit it. But it ran away, it came to see me, it couldn't understand why I had no voice, no hands. I heard it coming from a long way off, leaping up on me, its eyes horror-stricken to find the little master to whom it had devoted its life mute and numb. Everyone spoke, everyone had hands to pet it, except for the one person it loved. All I could do for it was pass in front of its gate sometimes, without seeming to see it, but talking, talking to my mother, saying: 'Mama, that's Flop, Flop kept me from writing you, I'll never pet Flop again.' Its name was a caress for the dog. It barked. It howled. It didn't know it was my remorse. Moreover, I never appreciated in its lifetime how sweet it is to have a remorse named Flop . . . Flop died from a snake-bite during a hunt. I never took Flop hunting, but I let the hunter who lived on the next estate hunt with him. Flop was so obedient that he never crawled under the fence onto my fields. I took him to the Château for a shot myself. It was too late."

Nelly wasn't listening. She was listening to the legend of her sufferings told by Fontranges: "Then Reginald disappeared, and Nelly waited for him. She expected him any minute, any second. Even in places and at times when Reginald had never come. She expected him at dawn, when the ragpickers open the garbage pails, she expected him at the couturier's, in her bath, at the chiropodist's. If she went to a railway station, she expected him at each train. If the wind moved the shutters, she expected him. If a hare ran across the road in front of the car, she expected him. And Reginald never appeared. She didn't expect him on the telephone, by telegraph, from the postman. But if the rain fell in floods, if the sun was merciless, she expected him . . . Nothing resembled Reginald, and everything reminded her of him. Everything was Reginald's presence in an implacable absence. He was not only changed into Tamar, her favorite mare, he was changed into everything which caught the eye, which struck the ear, and even, when she ate, which suddenly roused the palate—for instance, an eclair. She knew the places where he was, where to see him, where to find him, but she avoided them, for searching is not expecting. She stopped drinking a glass of wine, for suddenly she was expecting him. If a beggar came toward her, she expected Reginald. If the day looked like an unmade bed, she expected him. When a clock struck the hour, she seemed to hear the hour and gave a start of expectation. She no longer gambled, she no longer read, she no longer swam, she expected . . . Sometimes she expected him as a bride would, embellishing herself, she would even have bought orange blossoms. Sometimes she expected him in the manner of a fisherman's wife: stubborn and fierce, ready to mumble a prayer and leave a candle on the altar . . . Sometimes she expected him like a guilty woman, aching with humiliation . . . Sometimes like a deceived wife, and then she expected Reginald in order to reproach him for this crime he had committed against her . . . But she never cried. At least she would never sink to complaints, nor to investigations, nor to tears."

That was what Fontranges was saying, in his silence. He said all that, and also he looked with infinite compassion at Nelly's face, a face that was smiling but suddenly wet with as many tears as if it had been raining tears and they had all been deposited on Nelly.

13

Nelly tried to figure how much harm she would do Fontranges if she were to marry him. For in the last few days she had noticed something: she was drawing Fontranges into a trap. Her old apprehension of other men, her fear they would propose to her—so intense that on the day Gaston actually did, she had almost screamed in terror—why did it now yield to Fontranges? Nelly wondered if this was another of her lies: was she trying to win Fontranges' friendship by lying about her lies, was she disguising certain vulgar deceptions by fantasy? She searched her past life for justifications, but as a matter of fact she had been precise just when children daydream, realistic when schoolgirls invent. Before Reginald, she had invented nothing. Her dolls remained dolls. The images on the wall never came down from their frames. Even in bed with fever, she stared at a ceiling that was always smooth, the bouquets on the wallpaper neither wilted nor bloomed.

She admired Lulu: at eleven, Lulu had had an imaginary dog, her faithful Bob. Bob slept with Lulu. She had to take him out three times a day. Sometimes he ran away, and they found Lulu sobbing in her bed because Bob had not come home. Lulu's mother had been forced to accept the fiction: in order to calm her daughter, she would take Bob to work with her, where he was a good dog or a bad dog depending on her moods, she took him on vacations to the Morvan, terrible vacations for Lulu, the countryside being full of vipers and Bob determined to dig for shrewmice. One day he even found truffles. And Lulu had become so concerned, so exigent about this nonexistent Bob, so much sweeter and kinder because of him that she had to be forgiven his non-existence, and one day Nelly had brought her a real Bob, imagining the child would be pleased. But the other Bob had subsisted, had prevailed; there had been terrible battles between the living dog and the imaginary one, and in order to separate them Lulu dealt out blows so equitably to both dogs that the real Bob had to be given away.

But for her whole life, Nelly, on the contrary, had heard only the voices everyone else heard too, and for her the night air, the mountain air was pure of phantoms and spirits. Then Reginald had come. And suddenly, just as her precision had become a kind of justice, her realism a kind of virtue, her selfishness a kind of purgation, so her lying had been ennobled, purified, had become a kind of imagination, and her hardness transformed to suffering. The voice which dictated her lies to her had changed . . . What did it mean that now, with Fontranges, it changed again, that she felt the need to lie away her lies? Did it mean she loved Fontranges too? Or was she going to have a different lie for each man she would ever meet?

The more she thought about Gaston and Reginald, the less she thought of freeing herself from them by a confession. Gaston would have forgiven her if she had written him the truth. But she would rather have been drawn and quartered than do so: this dreadful, uncertain atmosphere was still more endurable than the truth. Reginald might have forgiven her, if she had confessed both her love and her lying. But a pride greater than her weakness forced her not to give in. If only she were put to one of those ancient tortures where the fire decides, where she would have had to accept the verdict of the red-hot iron in order to prove she had told the truth when she told Reginald that she was married to an ancient uncle, that she had a chateau in the Aube, that she was rich and chaste. She would have let herself be abused by the torturer, broiled and grilled until it was the judges who were put in the wrong by the very excesses of her suffering and her obduracy. She would not confess. If Reginald were to come and ask if she had lied, she would say no, despite all the proofs to the contrary. She would rather lose everything than be in the wrong. Her honor was to deny the charge against all evidence, against all interest. Let him come! She would insist she had been a virgin. Moreover, the torture existed. It took place almost every minute, but especially at nightfall. Why not during the hours when Reginald and Nelly used to meet? That would have been more natural, more tolerable. No. During those hours, on the contrary, there was a sudden kind of insensitivity in her, it was as if her tension had lowered, as if her power to suffer or to love had been reduced. The hours in which one has suffered too much are like the places where one has danced too much, marched too much. Nothing grows there any more. That those splendid afternoon hours might someday be fertile again was a question which in any case had not yet come up. For now, they were a sterile slope up to the twilight.

The day had suddenly lengthened, there was too much of it; Nelly filled those hours the way you fill an embankment with slag, with all kinds of uninteresting occupations, with swimming, with movies, with Spanish lessons. Since the age of twelve, she had not had time to learn Spanish. Now there was time. The Spanish teacher, moreover, was not deceived: it seemed to him quite suspect that at her age Nelly showed so much eagerness even after the lesson on the verbs *ser* and *estar,* that she never cancelled a lesson. But all the other hours of the day, the hours which had had almost nothing of Reginald, demanded him, desired him, as though he were demanded and desired in Nelly herself by a host of thoughts and feelings he had never touched. Why should the morning of the anniversary of the Battle of the Marne, why should noon on Armistice Day, why should Nelly's pleasure in buying shoes—why should there be clamoring for Reginald? It was neither because of war nor peace nor because of her unquestionable need to own fifty pairs of shoes, but Reginald's absence was unendurable. Morning and night, separated by this imperceptible catwalk, were stripped bare; in each dream she wakened from a dreadful reality; in each wakening, from an exhausting dream. It was all too obvious: the only life to live was between dream and waking, was life with Reginald. Where was he vulnerable? There had to be a realm, a sector where vision, reasoning, imagination would make it possible to approach him. Vengeance was simple: to prove he had been wrong, to prove she had not lied to him, to meet him only on the day she would be what he had believed she was; when she would be rich, honored, wife of a noble, sovereign being, married yet chaste, when she would be married to Fontranges . . .

That was what she thought about, now, at night. She scrutinized this plan of hers: by marrying Fontranges was she merely seeking advantages for herself? Marrying Fontranges was a noble thing to do only if she did it for Reginald. She was afraid to discover that this was not entirely the case, that there was room in her life for a third state. She realized that if she asked her mother for advice—the most selfish inspiration to be found—her mother would advise her to marry Fontranges, and insofar as such a marriage meant giving Fontranges a mother-in-law, it was in fact abominable. If Fontranges were not himself—if he were old Prince Demodoff, ruined and corrupt, who asked nothing better than to revise destiny, or if he were old Monsieur Moïse, the ugly banker who seemed to have a penchant for Nelly—would she have envisaged the project with the same complacency? There was no lack of princely old men disposed to take Nelly for their wife. No. For it seemed to her that only with Fontranges did she enter a kind of legend—with the others she continued in reality. If she did not somehow lead Reginald into that realm where the imaginary truth prevails over the factual one, she was defeated from the start.

What most amazed Nelly was to discover that though she had always lived from day to day, though she had had only each day's appetite, though she had thought, in her affair with Reginald, only of the hour she would spend with him, and at the hour's end of the minute, the last minute when she gave all of herself, the minute when Reginald was just about to get out of the car—what most amazed Nelly now was that she no longer thought of those brief joys, of the day's diversion, but of her future life. She no longer had the impiety of happiness which leads to tasting it piecemeal. She had found her religion of happiness. There was a paradise on earth, one which might come in a few years: all of life with Reginald. The afternoon with Reginald—that might be deserved quite easily, might even be obtained now by tempting Reginald, by all those instruments which are the auxiliaries of temptation, the telephone, the letter, the message, the telegram. She decided that if she were to try to get Reginald back, she could do it, but only by supplication, by revealing her deceptions, by a horrible admission of the lie of her life. While all of life with Reginald could be won much more arduously, but much more certainly. It was not a matter of winning an hour of clamorous joy with Reginald, but of breakfasting in bed with Reginald, the right to butter his toast beside him in smooth sheets, in sight of everyone—chambermaids, hotel managers . . . It was not a matter of shrieking into Reginald's ear that she adored him, but of placidly waiting for him on some villa terrace. It was a matter of being without desire, without passion. Nelly was obsessed to the point of tears, of wringing her hands, with that almost neutral, almost insipid state. It was a matter of being with Reginald the way she was with Fontranges. And since death had to come someday, it was not a matter, when she died, of Reginald suddenly appearing, pale and pathetic, summoned by Eglantine, among the tearful family, but of Reginald sitting beside her all the while, quite comfortable in that mortuary bedroom; as comfortable, of course, as a man can be who is going to kill himself as soon as Nelly breathes her last, for she had no doubt he would do what she herself was quite determined to do once Reginald's eyes were closed forever. It was a matter of entering a life, a long life whose last day would be the last day for both of them. In any case, that was the only way to make all of today's sufferings . . . sufferable: to believe they were a preparation for happiness.

But on certain days it really was insufferable. On certain days she had her doubts. She suddenly discovered that her reasoning was correct, that her labor of two years, three years—she allowed whatever was necessary to win Reginald back—was effective only on one condition: that Reginald did not change. She had counted on everything: on her own persistence, on her virtue, on her love, on the possibility of transforming the future into the past, and she was absolutely sure of it all. But the habit she had acquired with Reginald, the habit of not questioning him about his life, had almost convinced her that he lived only during the hours he was with her. Afterwards he dissolved, he melted into Paris, and her share of him then was no more than atoms and air. It was this certainty she had come to and lived on since their separation: Reginald was nowhere, he did not exist when he was not with her. He was in the limbo women believe their lovers inhabit when they are not in their beds. Nelly, of course, knew that Reginald was not totally dissolved, but for her he lived a secondary life, a life in which the vital operations—lunch, a shower, sleep—were performed languidly; the life of a queen bee retired from the duties and dangers of existence. That was what life meant for so many women: an existence in which women are terribly alive and busy from morning to night while the larvae of lovers, gently bathed, fed and warmed in the sun, wait for the hours of love to come round again.

Now it suddenly occurred to her, one morning, that she could no longer count on an unalterable Reginald. She understood in a flash of revelation that

Reginald, like other men, crossed the street, was exposed to automobile accidents, banana peels, to the miasmas of typhoid or hay fever. She suddenly saw him —Reginald, hitherto created out of an immortal and impregnable substance—breathing, panting; she saw him talking to other men, to other women, to another woman, and heading at one and the same time toward death and toward another affection.

O Lord, how terrible Fontranges' legend became! She could hear its echoes: "Now she realized that Reginald would never have been changed into Tamar. Tamar, a descendant of the horses of the Prophet, was certainly an incarnation, but merely an incarnation of the fidelity to forms. Reginald had been changed into nothing, if not into Reginald. He awakened, dressed, ordered the car, negotiated with the rulers of Europe, had himself shaved by a barber, had his hangnails trimmed by a manicurist—he talked to that manicurist, he asked her if she liked the theatre, liked the country —he bought a newspaper, he spoke to the woman in the newspaper kiosk: he asked her if she was taking a vacation, and where. Then he worked, and around five, his afternoons being free, being a desert, he visited aunts and cousins. He spoke to the prettiest ones. He asked them if they liked the theatre, liked the country, and where they would take their vacation. He spoke to them: speaking to a woman consists in moving the lips and the tongue while looking at her and reading in her eyes which movements are to be given to that tongue and those eyes. He danced with them: dancing with a woman consists in taking her in your arms and embracing her in time to the music which carries you both into empty corners and window niches."

That was Reginald's life now. Every day he was changing. Every day he was forgetting. Every day he was moving farther away. Ah, suddenly she felt the misery of loving a man! How much safer it would have been to love God! Sometimes she saw Reginald's hair growing as she watched, then whitening, she saw his shoulders stooping, bent by age. Suddenly she was ready to run toward him, to reach him before he was deaf and dumb with age. One day she ran.

She waited for him at the entrance to a lecture hall, behind the thin hedge of plainclothesmen whose duty was to applaud the famous foreign minister. She waited the way you wait for the couple to pass by in a wedding. From far away she saw him coming, with his tranquil, lofty gait: she closed her eyes, she almost collapsed, and luckily it wasn't Reginald at all, it was a short, fat man with a nervous, sidelong step. Then she saw him again, with his face held high, his long gloveless hands, and again it wasn't Reginald, it was a man with his head down, his stubby fingers in pigskin gloves. Within ten minutes all these contrary specimens of humanity came out of an image of Reginald—which opened up within range of her voice and left them there—as though out of an egg. And finally, when almost the entire swarm of false Reginalds she could create had been engulfed by the lecture hall, the true Reginald appeared. Old age had not touched him. He was miraculously preserved from cataracts, from paralysis. A slight melancholy covered him, like a raincoat, which kept ordinary life from disfiguring him, from staining him. No one was with him. He really seemed to be coming from that invisible and non-existent realm from which he used to come to Nelly, that realm without women, without appetites, without age. He passed without seeing her. Hidden behind a broad-shouldered plainclothesman who was serving for the first time as a screen for love and who shouted "Viva Rumania!" into Reginald's face, Nelly almost fainted as she leaned against the plainclothesman's powerful arm, smitten by the kind of death which her lover's indifferent passage inflicted upon her, and by the kind of fidelity this proof of his permanence afforded. That he should be the same, that to the naked eye he should seem not to have changed—that was the best proof Reginald could give of his love!

Nelly went home, she had a moment's respite. But it was a short moment, and as soon as she went to bed, it came to an end. She had the impression she had seen only an appearance; she had seen Reginald only from six feet away. From six feet away, the past resembles the present, sickness resembles health. Perhaps there was a white hair beside each hair: perhaps this entity which seemed the same really consisted of a thousand tiny wrinkles. She should have examined Reginald at six inches, from as close as eyes can get, she should have touched him, caressed him from as close as a mouth can come. Why wasn't there some other means of knowing the lover who is avoiding you, some other means than the means which serve to know the lover who loves you: to take him in your arms. In the middle of the night Nelly wakened, horrified: Reginald had grown old, old the way Fontranges was old. And Fontranges too aged before her eyes. She had to hurry with Fontranges. Otherwise she would find herself in the world with no means of ever escaping from this dilemma in which she had imprisoned herself.

14

Starting the morning when the society columns announced Nelly's engagement to Fontranges, there were, on the part of fate, first timid and then more vigorous attempts to fall in with Nelly's plans. Gaston sent back Nelly's letters, which were burned. Lulu found an old charcoal-burning foot warmer, the kind no longer used except for suicides, and Nelly burned the letters, stirring them—first red, then ashen—with a poker. Then Gaston managed to fall out of a plane and lose part of his memory. Nelly was informed of the accident. She wasn't certain which she preferred: being in the surviving part, or in the dead part. She went to see him. He failed to recognize her. They told him she was a cousin, he believed everything they told him, he believed she was a cousin, and Gaston was gentle and kind with her, the way he was with cousins. As a matter of fact, the memory women have of the men who have loved them must be the same as the memory men have of women, for when she saw Gaston, Nelly not only remembered nothing about him, about them, but felt nothing. At seeing Gaston's eyes discovering her, his face knowing nothing about her, his hands touching her hands as if she were a new woman, a fierce and terrible virginity recurred in her body. A terrible jealousy, too, of this Gaston who had just been reborn, who no longer bore the stigmata of his past life. Where was the plane which could deposit her that way, at the side of a road, among trees and faces which would be the first trees and the first faces of her life, and which would allow her to reappear before Reginald—for she would remember Reginald—without reticence, all her secrets lost to herself, buried in an unconscious body. She took a lot of observation flights that month. Of course she wasn't counting on a miracle of that kind, but you never know . . . The handsome pilots who took her in their arms to install Nelly in their little planes never dreamed that this young client was seeking, from them, a virginity.

Then one fine day, Fontranges made a move.

*

* *

"Is it very urgent?" Reginald's secretary asked Fontranges. "Monsieur Reginald is very eager not to keep you waiting in any case. But at any moment the Franco-Iraqi friendship treaty is to be signed in his office."

Fontranges smiled. He had the impression that what he was there to find out had a more urgent character than any friendship being sealed between Paris and Bagdad. Suppose a physician, an otologist, is about to sign the Franco-Prussian friendship pact, and that a child must have an emergency mastoid operation. I believe that the negotiators would not hesitate, especially if the child were the son of one of them.

"Very urgent."

The secretary showed him into the office where Reginald was reading over, with an attaché, the last articles of the treaty. The secretary gave him a chair. Fontranges looked at the treaty. He had never seen a treaty, even from a distance. He was rather disappointed. Even from a distance, a treaty should be bright colored, the scrolls attached by tricolor ribbons, with huge illuminated initials which have so much to do with conciliation and friendship. From his chair, Fontranges saw no more than a typed document, the sheets paper-clipped together. Harun al-Rashid would not have been satisfied.

Then Fontranges looked at Reginald. He was a man, obviously. Not a happy man. A certain clarity enveloped him. But cold. The clarity of former happiness. Fontranges would have been warmer about signing a friendship pact with Iraq. No. Nelly had certainly made a mistake. This distant man with his polite smile was not Tamar. Tamar would have pranced at signing a friendship pact with real Arab horses, with camels, with the huge hares which leap up under your feet in the ruins of Babylon. Reginald certainly impressed Fontranges as a man who would always have difficulties in establishing friendship with Karbala or with Mosul, and above all with the cities of the past, with Nineveh. This was terribly apparent at first glance, especially with regard to the past! With all his being, Reginald denied the past. He seemed to think Fontranges had been in his office since eternity.

"I'm quite at your disposition," he said, coming toward him. "They'll probably interrupt us, but don't be alarmed."

Fontranges cast about for some device which would allow him to make the transition from this Arab treaty to the conversation about Nelly. There was certainly one. To mention Tamar; but it was so increasingly obvious that this man was not Tamar that he gave it up . . . Why are the men who must sign friendship treaties the men who are coldest and most reticent? Fontranges knew so many men who would have signed this one with emotion, with warmth. He was ready to sign one with Reginald. Moreover that was what he had come for: a treaty of understanding between men, between those conventions which are time and reality.

"I'm getting married," Fontranges said.

A shadow passed over Reginald's face. There could be no doubt that this notion of marriage displeased him. It was not because of Fontranges. It was because marriage presupposes a woman, and because he was perfectly willing to hear about anything, to discuss anything, but not women. "I congratulate you," he said.

"I'm marrying Nelly," Fontranges said.

The chief of protocol came in to arrange the ceremony. Not for a moment did he seem to think Fontranges' presence could be detrimental to the signing of the treaty. Fontranges did not think so either. Already Reginald was coming back toward him. "I congratulate you twice over."

"Monsieur," Fontranges said, "I see your question on your lips: 'How does this concern me?' Monsieur, you are not sincere, or you do not take a proper view of your personal life. It concerns you insofar as your happiness concerns you, insofar as happiness is superior to unhappiness. I am marrying the woman who loves you, the woman you love, and you have nothing to say to me?"

"I don't understand you."

"Say her name first. Don't hesitate to say her name when it appears in your sentence. You are formal and constrained, not because you do not want to speak about her, but because you have vowed never to utter her name."

Reginald looked harder at Fontranges. It was true, as a matter of fact. For these three months the struggle had been less against the thought, the vision of Nelly than against her name. It had been a matter of living, not by eliminating all memory of her but by eliminating her name. Her name was like an insoluble part of that love which—so stubborn was Reginald—would otherwise have dissolved. He could see without suffering too much, he could listen or speak without suffering too much, but as soon as the name appeared, rose to his lips, to his ears, everything went wrong. He had weaned himself from it the way you wean yourself from alcohol, from tobacco. He had reached the point of hearing other men pronounce that name without too much pain. Finally he imagined he had deprived her of her name. She slept without a name. She got up, bathed, breakfasted without a name. It was difficult for the memory, for desire to cling to this nameless entity which almost became once more one of those unreal women who had haunted the youth of a chaste and scholarly Reginald. She was a temptation, a still-dazzling apparition, but unapproachable because of that namelessness. Often, at night, she had appeared in his sleep, so close but fluttering, trying to recover her name, to regain ground, nameless, trying the names of all the saints who might have been her sponsors, vainly seeking that name which would give her back her own. Reginald waited, saw her, felt the name in his mouth like a seed, waited cruelly until she had left again, suffering, ready to follow the man who would have given her any name, ready to fling herself upon Reginald if he had called her Jeanne, or Ursule, or Miriam. But he kept these names back too. He uttered no woman's name. No, he would not utter it in front of Fontranges. For Nelly—my God, what was happening to his mind! —would appear.

"Let us speak frankly," Fontranges said.

He wants me to speak frankly, Reginald was thinking, because he wants to find out about Nel . . . about her. She lies to him the way she lied to me, and to the other one, who is perhaps ten others. What does speaking frankly mean to the man who is going to marry a woman with whom you have slept two hundred times, who has undressed in front of you two hundred times, who has sworn that she loves you alone, that everything in her life is meaningless except for you, that your kisses are, as that Arab coming in to sign his damn treaty would say, like unto spices and myrrh, that your words are even as the lute and the viol, that your heart is the steed of Mohammed at a trot, and that she would kill herself if she ever missed a single day, a single hour of your lovemaking. Which comes to seventy-three days, fifteen hours, if I am reckoning correctly, and forty-five or forty-eight minutes. She has not killed herself and is about to marry an old man. A handsome old man. So let us speak frankly. Let us tell him that she has never been anyone's mistress, much less mine, that I have never come closer than six inches to her, that she is candid and faithful.

"Nelly loves you," Fontranges said. "I know what you have been to each other. I also have the impression that you love her. Let us speak frankly."

What does he want, Reginald was wondering. Does he want me to promise never to see her again? Agreed. Or does he want me to promise to come and see her? To come and see her as an old friend, as an indifferent man, without seeing her?

"Come in!"

The man who came in was the Iraqi plenipotentiary, Ali Bey, a direct descendant of Harun al-Rashid, as Reginald informed Fontranges when he introduced them. The friendship treaty was read aloud. The presence of Fontranges, toward whom Ali Bey turned with a smile from time to time—in fact, each time the word friendship was pronounced—seemed not only natural but necessary to its success, though he had nothing more to do with it than the pebble dropped into the pot of broth in the fable. He seemed responsible for giving flavor to this treaty: these were really signatures of friendship. The French minister signed on the left, from left to right according to Latin script, then Ali Bey signed on the right, from right to left, as if he were coming closer with each syllable. Then the Arabs and the chief of protocol left. Ali Bey had taken Fontranges' hands in his own. Since the Third Crusade, there had not been such an embrace between the Arabs and the Fontranges.

"And you—do you love Nelly?" Reginald had spoken the name. He realized it from the fact that his ears suddenly hummed, that his eyes filled with tears.

"I love her," Fontranges said. "I could never have imagined a more charming grand-niece to lead me to death. Don't you agree?"

No, I don't agree, Reginald was thinking. To die in the company of someone who has secrets, to leave the earth in order to abandon secrets—that was scarcely tempting. For the first time he felt that among the reasons he had for living, there was this one: to learn

Nelly's secrets, or at least to be contemporary with Nelly's secrets. And that was all. This splendid old gentleman had come to tell him that he knew Reginald had been his wife's lover. Fine. That would avoid a certain embarrassment if they happened to meet at an exhibition of nudes at Saint-Moritz or at the Dijon museum. The three of them, with a few polite phrases, could visit the tomb of Philippe of Burgundy. They could talk in loud voices about the dog keeping watch at Philippe's feet, pretending to laugh at the dog while Fontranges would be thinking of the bliss of lying down that way too, joined soon by his own dog that would live only ten years, and finally, after fifty, by Nelly, by young Nelly old and decrepit, whose bones would break as they laid her beside him.

"Why don't you want to see Nelly again?"

"Didn't she tell you?"

"She told me you thought she was a lying woman."

"She lies the way she breathes."

"Did she lie inside what was your life?"

What is he getting at? Reginald wondered. Is he trying to convince himself he's leading an honest woman to the altar? Does he also want to reconstruct her virginity? I think that would probably be easier.

"Monsieur," Fontranges said, "I don't think I've ever told a lie in my life. But I would not swear that my life as a whole is as true as Nelly's. Let us admit she lies the way she breathes. In any case, there has formed in her existence a kind of jewel: out of all that lying, she has secreted a pearl, an absolute truth which was her love for you. Between those walls where you met, within that terrible emotion which has so belabored and exhausted you both, did she lie? Did she ever make a single gesture which was a lie? Let me say this: it is you who made her lie. Just as it is you who chose the apartment, it is you who told this charming and passionate woman what she should be when she was not with you. Never did you question her, never did you hear her confession. You had the opportunity of receiving the devotion of a soul eager to be rid of the encumberments with which God burdens at birth girls of ordinary circumstances—compromise and indifference. Never once did you help her. God knows what impelled you to prefer, to this woman rooted so deep in life, nourished upon a bourgeois reality, a mannequin cut off from the world by birth, by fortune and by marriage. She was the daughter of middle-class people, she was poor, she was unmarried. It is you who obliged her, quite unconsciously, to deny all that. What wouldn't she have done for you, who desired, the moment you left her, to be leaving one of the forces of the world rather than one of its flaws? What must it have cost her to become, during the moment you stared after her from the taxi driving you away, what you wanted her to be? She would have made herself, just as cheaply, into a millionairess and a queen. And after all, that is what you wanted."

"Perhaps."

"That is what you wanted. Not that there is the slightest vanity in your case. But you believe nonetheless that great loves are made only out of great souls. The love of a Nelly who was a millionairess and a queen seemed to you the minimum. I had a friend like you. He was, unfortunately, slightly deaf. He and I were sergeants major in the Saint-Germain dragoons, and he wanted to love only queens. He was a handsome fellow, and down to the day he was promoted to the rank of regimental sergeant at Saumur, he kept his word. The queens he loved were the wives of the captain and the colonel who were his superior officers. But when he left Saint-Germain he was tired of it. Their husbands the kings were idiots. Their daughters the princesses—except for one or two who would be future queens—pretentious and narrow-minded. Their sons the princes, contentious as to the margin which separates heirs apparent from assistant brigadiers in the dragoons. The queens themselves were enthusiastic enough—not very good about hats, he said—more enthusiastic than he, since they selected, under the king's nose, a young non-com—then came demands that Commander O., General O.'s father, ask Colonel de la Colovrière . . . In short, the atmosphere became so bad he finally obliged the queens to say no more about their family connections and to become no more than mannequins in the Rue de la Paix. When they did so, they became utterly charming. But I digress . . ."

Is he right? Reginald wondered. He's wrong. If I thought of Nelly that way, I did it so that she would be born for me. From nobility, from wealth, I saw her born the way Venus is born, not from a suburb, but from the waves and the sunlight. Every evening, when I left her, I saw her return, not to a sordid and greedy life, but dissolve, melt into the twilight or the night. To imagine Nelly that way, an almost non-existent Nelly, was the only way I could endure her absence. She was leaving me for an unconscious life, rich in radium and gold. Oh, how she seemed to be returning to Donatellos and Rembrandts, at the very moment she was returning to her trivial woman's apartment! She lies the way she breathes . . . Every woman lies the way she breathes.

Fontranges had stood up. The story of the assistant brigadier had evidently led him a little beyond his subject. "I see," he said, "that you have no idea of what I am proposing. Perhaps you will understand better if I tell you that within two weeks Nelly will be my wife."

As a matter of fact, Reginald had no idea.

"And if I show you her future calling cards, will you have an idea? I have just had them engraved. They are a little . . . imaginative. Look."

Reginald read: Nelly, Marquise de Fontranges.

"You still have no idea? You feel nothing?"

Yes, he felt something. A kind of shock. A kind of memory. Reading, seeing that new name reminded him of some unidentified happiness, of some past peace. Now he had it: the first day he had met Nelly.

"Now," Fontranges said, "you have it. She will also be a baroness—Baronne de Charlemagne. She will be what you thought she was, what you had made her say she was, what permitted you to love her. You understand now, don't you?"

What I understand comes straight out of the cinema, Reginald was thinking. I understand that Nelly is making amends. I understand that she is expiating her lying. I understand that she wants to appear before me some day, when not one of the things she told me will be false. "And Gaston?" he asked.

"Gaston has lost his memory."

"And the others? There were others."

"One is dead. The other is nothing."

"And her mother? Her dreadful mother!"

"Unfortunately her mother is alive. There is nothing to be done about that. It must be admitted that the woman is indestructible. Apparently she likes travel and wood carvings—we'll send her to Colombo."

"And her lying when she says she doesn't know some man and then she leaves your arms to go to his?" I understand, Reginald was thinking, that this loyal and honest Fontranges thinks that there has been no lying if the lie is made good—that from a certain altitude it doesn't matter much whether words are confirmed by the past or by the future. He doesn't know how to express himself, but I believe he means that he's going to marry Nelly, that he's going to erase all the lies she told me, or that he's going to make them come true, so that I'll see her again and respect her. "If I understand you correctly," Reginald said to Fontranges, "you don't want Nelly to have been a lying woman. You are marrying her so that she will be what she said she was. From the day she becomes your wife, if I should meet her one afternoon, and if she spoke to me, and if she loved me, everything she told me six months ago would be true."

"That is why she is marrying me."

"She wants to have told me the truth? She knows she has told me a filthy lie!"

"Has she been so mistaken? When God has given a child certain tastes and certain desires, who is the more consistent—God or the child—if the only way the child can realize them is by not accepting other people's truth?"

"If a woman had made Gaston believe she was a queen when she was not a queen, what would Gaston have said?"

"It has happened. The daughter of a records clerk in Brive has made Gaston believe precisely that. She is now his wife."

"Very well. I shall see, on the day of your wedding, how I feel."

"That will be the twenty-fourth, and today is already the eighteenth."

"Does that matter?"

"Then you still don't understand, my poor boy! Your happiness—Nelly's happiness is yours—is at stake between now and then! Each of us bears only one truth in life. A painter can lie, he has the truth of color. A rancher can lie, he is true among his steers. What we call specialization in the arts or sciences is nothing but truth. The fact that a diviner lies with regard to magpie nests is a matter of little consequence, provided he tells the truth with regard to springs. Nelly's truth is her love for you. What does life prove to you today? That the false garment in which Nelly dressed for you can become, if you absolutely insist on it, a true one. Do you need it that much?"

"I should prefer it to have been true then."

"I'm afraid you are a little hard. You must not be hard on any contemporary, man or woman, animal or insect. It is so astounding, in this leakage of thousands of centuries, that they should have found means of being on the earth at the same time as you. It is really a series of appointments, miraculously kept, in spite of rapes, floods, and eclipses. They are appointments, you know—appointments with kindness, malice, beauty, ugliness, but appointments, promises, understandings. Nelly was determined to keep her promise. She has been atom, dust, fetus with incredible perseverance, slowing down when you slowed down as a starfish, accelerating when you accelerated in a cloud of microbes. She is still here. The appointment stands. She is aging only at your own speed. She takes from the sun only the complexion which darkens you every day. She eats your food, drinks your water and your wines. She did not have an appointment with me. Why do you force her to make one? I implore you, come and take her before the wedding. I lunch and dine with her every day. We expect you. I'll leave word, if we should go to the Bagatelle or to the theatre."

He held out his hand to Reginald. For the scene

to be perfect, the ushers should have come in singing in chorus, the doors should have burst open of their own accord, and the Arab signatories should have accompanied Fontranges to his house on horseback . . . But Reginald did not have the gift. If such a thing took place, he saw nothing.

*

* *

Reginald was wondering why he didn't obey Fontranges. It was not because he doubted Nelly's love. He was sure of it. He was sure of it the way he was sure of one of the pillars of the world. He felt it was one of the future elements of his life. Nelly loved him, he needed that love—if Nelly had told the truth in the past and if she no longer loved him now he would not have traded such a solution for the present one. And he loved Nelly too. No other woman distracted him from her. He felt her so close to him, so close behind him that he never turned around. And he dreamed of her. And at night, Reginald who never talked in his sleep discovered that he spoke of Nelly. Moreover Nelly's past was a matter of indifference to him. And he realized too that he had been right: she was the liveliest woman in the world, the most valiant, the most faithful. And he had a vision of life with Nelly, a simple life in a villa near Paris, with all those plants of Saint-Cloud or of Bougival which had kept the appointments Fontranges was talking about. And he felt the happiness springing up everywhere in that life the way water leaks into a boat, irresistibly—a shipwreck of happiness. And he attached no more importance in itself to Nelly's lying, he forgave it, it didn't deserve to arouse either disapproval or hatred. And his hat was on the table for him to go to Nelly. And his topcoat was on the chair. And the car downstairs was waiting to take him to Nelly. And the streets opened before him for this very purpose. And everything was prologue to his arrival. In each morning, each afternoon, there was some historical solution or fluid which could in a single gesture dye forever the entire past, and Paris, and his house, and the day itself. All the marvelous souvenirs of reconciliation stirred under a series of minor events or minor apparitions which would be, if he persisted, only nothingness. Nor was it that he wanted to make Nelly suffer. But he didn't mind her suffering because he was adding this suffering of Nelly's to his own, so that the more Nelly suffered, the more her suffering, thus enlarged within himself, justified her, absolved her. Apparently she cried a lot. Those tears wrested from Nelly gave her a kind of sanctity, a kind of martyrdom.

No. What he felt was only a kind of sulkiness. But Nelly's lying—you admit all the lies, even the worst ones, you forgive them, you forgive the poor creatures who have told them, that's not the question—Nelly's lying had offended something in Reginald which was neither sensibility nor intelligence, had withered an organ which did not revive, which did not grow back.

O Nelly, he wasn't angry with you any more because of your lying. And Fontranges was right, and you were right, since you were going to be—since you *could* be Madame de Fontranges. But there was that deathblow given by your pathetic and charming and lovable lying to what was neither heart nor brain. It was as if the lying attacked not the emotions but the viscera. Every specialist of the spleen, the bile duct, would have had to be consulted to discover the nature of this incurable disease. That was the trouble with lies: you could make them come true, you could make them beautiful, they could become a splendor, but they provoked in Reginald that terrible indisposition against which he was helpless, a kind of rancor, and though lying became pure, brilliant, even became in his eyes an act of kindness, of love, the unknown organ suffered, gave him nausea.

15

"He won't come," Nelly said.

"Are you waiting for someone?" Nelly's mother asked Fontranges.

"We're not waiting for him, we just expect him," Nelly said. "Only I don't expect him."

"I do."

"May one be informed who it might be?" the mother asked.

"No. No one can know. No one can suspect that we are waiting for him here, that we are expecting him. No one can imagine that the two of us are here, not expecting him but supposing he might come. You would fall down dead if you knew whom we were talking about."

"That's not true! You would tell me right away."

"You're in no danger. He won't come."

"It's a man, in any case. Is he . . . presentable?"

"Is he presentable, Fontranges?"

"He certainly is. He's the most presentable man I know."

"Put on your hat, Nelly. You're late already. I really don't like you in that black dress."

Fontranges had gone out—to speak to Eglantine, he said; actually, to see if Reginald was coming.

"Why wouldn't you wear white?"

"Because I've had a lover."

"Why do you speak that way to your own mother?"

"Because my mother doesn't love me, and because I hate her."

"Why do you feel the need to say such stupid things today?"

"Because today I want to see what the truth is. I want to feel it in my mouth. I want to hold it in my hand. I want the truth to touch me."

"My poor child!"

"Go away! Don't touch me!"

Fontranges had returned. "We must leave now, Nelly. You ride with Eglantine."

Nelly smiled. My God, how hard life is, and how funny, and dreadful, and comical. Hard for those who try to give it a chance to be soft and intelligent. In the last six days, Fontranges and Nelly had perpetrated every ruse known to man or child in order to keep, in each of their hours, their minutes, their seconds, a door through which Reginald could return. Not one sentence was spoken between them which might not have ended the drama with dignity and amity. Nelly's sleep was fitful, and there was a night light in the bedroom, and the key was never turned in the lock, so that Reginald could come at night, find his way in the dark around Nelly's bed. Every night when Fontranges went to bed, on the contrary, he left orders that he be wakened late, that his suitcase be packed, and a timetable be bought —all useful precautions if Nelly were to telephone him that the marriage was off, that Reginald had come. They made no travel plans. They took their meals in places where Reginald would normally have come to find them, obvious enough so that he would see them, but not too obvious, so that he would not be intimidated. Never was a trap laid more cunningly, never was life given a more splendid opportunity to forget its fatality and to show a little imagination.

Fontranges remembered that as a boy of seven, there had been a week just like this one: the week when he had arranged everything in and around himself so that the famous white doe the gamekeepers had told him about could come and make friends with him. During that week, just like Nelly now, not only did he not lock the door—you cannot ask of a doe what you can normally ask of Reginald, to turn the handle—but he left it ajar; and he also left the chateau gate open, and in the morning he would look for footprints, and there was even a rug spread with fresh hay beside the bed, so that if he was asleep the doe could eat her fill. For you cannot ask of a doe what you are entitled to ask of a lover, that he keep standing beside the bed looking at you, so that your first glance should touch his face. It was with his hand that little Fontranges, waking, groped for the adored fur beside his bed; he stretched out his arm, for there was nothing beside the bed, and finally he touched the rug still covered with hay. She had not come. She never came. Cats had come, dogs, once a horse had climbed the stairs all by itself. The delegate of the forest, of the countryside, of the inhabitants of that world which was the world of Fontranges, had never come, through any door, open or closed.

Only Nelly had come by that path reserved for a female quadruped with delicate hooves, tender nostrils, and a white belly. Henceforth Nelly would lie down beside him, intact. For Reginald, too, would doubtless never come. All the human beings and all the animals for which we create, in our summary and limited lives, bridges and breaches so that they will escape, remain instead gathered at the center of a Grail more fenced about by the air than by giant palings, and imagine themselves its prisoners.

"We must go down now," Fontranges said.

He was thinking that he should have gone looking for the white doe, should have captured it by lasso or snare, tied its hooves together, muzzled its mouth; should have done everything Nelly should have done, this week, to Reginald . . .

Now they were sitting side by side in front of their *prie-Dieu* in the church of Saint-Roch. All the traps laid on the road between the house and the *mairie,* even the final trap between the mayor's question—did he consent to take her for his wife—and its converse had turned out to be empty. The organ pealed out. They could speak quite clearly without being overheard. Fontranges, facing the altar, spoke to Nelly whose head was slightly bent.

"No," Nelly said.

"I won't mind. Stand up. Leave the Church. Go to him."

"I am your wife. I love you."

"You are not my wife, not yet before God. You are my wife before those civil authorities which will give you your freedom whenever you want it. You don't love me. You have an affection for me which I will feel however far away you are, moreover we will see each other, we will see each other often. You know perfectly well I cannot live without you—you are everything for me. You are my joy, my jewel, my youth. Now go, leave me!"

"No," Nelly's head said. But the movements of a bride's head are clearer than her words. And her smile. For a smile had come to her lips. "No," she said.

"You don't want to take Reginald for your husband?"

"No," she said. It was a ceremony exactly the opposite of the one the priest was performing.

"You love Reginald, Nelly. Reginald loves you. He's young. You have your life with him, and every happiness. This morning, you still agreed to it."

"Now I am your wife."

"Not yet. There's been a mistake. I was mistaken to try to console you, to save you by this means. Happiness in this world is caught by the stupidest bait, like the salmon by worms. We've been too subtle for it, too fastidious. Go to Reginald. I am your father."

"That is the only happiness I can still have: to marry my father."

These are either very pious or very garrulous newlyweds, the priest was thinking, who in his efforts to understand them was officiating one step behind the place he usually stood. Perhaps, moreover, they were not talking to God but to each other. Was it their last duet, or their first scene?

Now they stood up. "Nelly darling," Fontranges said, a little louder, for his mouth, when he was standing, was twice as far from Nelly's ear, "don't listen to this moment in yourself, the moment which enslaves us once a ceremony has begun. A wedding is obviously a solemnity, but this one is your own, you can interrupt it. The scandal is a minor one, there are not more than twenty of us here. Perhaps he will not come now. I cannot turn around. Neither can you. But just stand up, call the priest, tell him: 'I love another man, I must leave.' After all, that's really why you didn't wear a white dress, admit it: so you could leave in the middle of the ceremony, so you could jump into a taxi without being ridiculous as a bride. Hurry, go now!"

They were kneeling. "No, my friend," Nelly said. "No, be still." She added: "It's hard, getting married. Don't talk about losing Reginald. It's this kneeling. My God, it's hard on the knees, even with the cushion!"

She hasn't knelt since childhood, Fontranges was

thinking. It takes about twenty years for knees not to feel kneeling as a torment. Dear Nelly, she's kneeling in front of me, for me. He continued: "Nelly, someone's walking into the church. Someone's coming. Someone's stopping . . . He's lost his nerve. Turn around."

"I will not turn around. I'm your wife."

"If it's Reginald, will you go to him?"

"No, I'm staying here. I'm your wife. Too bad for him. Too bad for us."

"I'm turning around." He turned around; it was certainly the first time that a Fontranges had turned around, during his marriage service. One of them, an old man too, who in 1677 had married Marguerite de Moulins, had fallen dead. But none had turned around. A useless turn, moreover: it was a boy with a cherub's face who had wandered in—no doubt in order to watch the wedding, leaning against a column. But it wasn't Reginald. Nor some angel to replace him: the column held fast, the vault did not collapse, the paving did not swallow them up. Nelly bent her head. This time she's praying, Fontranges decided.

This time she was praying. "O my lord and master, my savior, help me, O Reginald darling, help me, come to me by not coming. Take me in your arms by not taking me. O Reginald humble of heart, my true light, my path, my counsel, my guide, deliver me by your pain, by your passion, deliver me. It's true that I must not go to you, isn't it? Everything I once told you is true now in the eyes of the civil authorities, it will be true in another moment in the eyes of God, in the eyes of Reginald. Farewell, you who loved me. Amen. Who raised me up to you like a rainbow. Amen. Who betrayed me, without explaining yourself, without showing yourself, for the ways of your providence are infinite. Amen. Who gave me this old friend to love, to polish with happiness until he tarnishes forever. Amen. Who abandoned me. Amen."

This time she's praying, the priest decided, and the husband too.

Which was not quite correct. By the sanctity of the place and the perfection of his soul, Fontranges was led, like Nelly, into a heresy. Thank you, he was thinking, Nelly darling. Thank you for your goodness, your kindness, your lying. You are right to trust me, to give yourself to me. At this moment there is taking place God knows what battle around us which will give us the victory. Seek out that victory, and then all will be well. If it is to forget Reginald, amen. If it is to go to Reginald, amen. Someone is walking into the church again, despite the presentation of the Holy Sacrament. But it's not Reginald, for he is stopping next to each guest. It's not Reginald peering under each hat to see which one is Nelly's. It's the Collection. But the priest is asking me a question. If I will take this woman for my wife, if I will cherish her, if I will give her protection and asylum . . . Yes.

It was as though he had gone deaf. He heard only a muffled *yes* beside him, like an echo. He decided that it wasn't fair, that it was a *yes* impressed by his own, that it was an echo. Would Nelly have said *no,* if she had spoken first?

There was a thin hedge of onlookers as they came out of the church. And Nelly caught a glimpse of Reginald, almost hidden behind one of them.

TRANSLATOR'S NOTE

La Menteuse was written in 1936, during one of Giraudoux' tours of duty as Inspector of Diplomatic and Consular Posts, in North and Central America. We can only speculate as to why he did not publish the book in his lifetime—a fragment of it was found among his papers after his death in 1944 and published in 1958; in 1968 an English scholar, Roy Prior, discovered the rest of the manuscript, and the entire novel was published in Paris in 1969—though the author's son is probably correct in assuming that the work was too intimate, too manifestly inspired by real persons, to appear in the follow-spots of literary and diplomatic attention by which Giraudoux was then regarded.

A generation after it was written, we are the more fortunate, not merely in having yet another work by "the Nijinsky of the novel," as Claude-Edmond Magny, his best critic, once called Giraudoux, but in having a work which, whatever its relation to "real" persons or events, has that sulfurous or seraphic aura which plays about texts of a certain—or uncertain—significance to their authors. In reference to Jane Austen, Henry James once said that she had the imagination of love, whereas he had the imagination of disaster. *Lying Woman* will be seen to have both kinds of imagination, and perhaps that is why we have had to wait so long for it, and why we are so fortunate to have it now.

Richard Howard